MW00778908

THE TRUTH
ACCORDING TO JOHN

A Metaphysical Mystery
of Revelation and Transformation

Pamala Oslie

OSLIE

OP

PRESS

SANTA BARBARA, CALIFORNIA

Books by Pamala Oslie

Life Colors: What the Colors in Your Aura Reveal

Love Colors: A New Approach to Love, Relationships, and Auras

Make Your Dreams Come True: Simple Steps for Changing the Beliefs that Limit You

Infinite You: Discover Your Quantum Powers, Parallel Universes, Spirituality, Telepathy, and More

Oslie Press
PO Box 30035
Santa Barbara, CA 93130

Editorial Reviews

"In this deeply felt story, Pamala Oslie brings life to one of our greatest mysteries of the spirit—and I can't thank her enough for that." --- Jeff Arch, Oscar nominated screenwriter, *Sleepless in Seattle,* and bestselling author

"This enlightening and riveting story will hold you till the last word and make you want more! It is a story that is certainly ready to be shared in these challenging times. It is hopeful, inspiring, thought-provoking, possibility driven and steeped in a deep understanding of spirituality and quantum physics. Brava Pamala Oslie!" ---Rod Lathim, Producer, Director, Author: *The Spirit of the Big Yellow House, Unfinished Business*

"The Truth According to John" touched me in a deeply, spiritual way. I found myself unable to put this story down, and, when finished...I wanted more. Pamala Oslie lifts the lid off of the reality box. I felt as though I was peeking inside of a what is possible and it allowed me to pivot and ponder my own thoughts on what I would like to see, hear, feel, and create as my own now. I sincerely hope this is an on-going series that keeps us spellbound for years to come." ---Jane Asher, podcast host and author of The Next Room

"This is a fascinating journey that will expand your mind and reshape your understanding of reality thanks to its profound insights. "---Irene Weinberg, Author of T*hey Serve Bagels in Heaven*, Host of Grief and Rebirth Podcast

PROLOGUE

Washington D.C. 1992. The lab was dark that night. A laser thin beam of light pierced the black. A scientist in a white lab coat, Dr. Martin, stood in front of a gray wall safe, a small flashlight in his hand. His back to the security camera, his broad shoulders shielded him from the roving eye. He anxiously fumbled with the combination lock.

Finally, Martin pulled open the reinforced steel door. He drew out a small black box. Inside was an old, discolored strand of fabric secured between two pieces of glass. He wrapped the fragile piece in a white cloth then slipped it into his pocket. He slid the empty black box back into the safe, locked the steel door and crept out.

5:00 am. Every light was on in the sterile lab. Only the open safe seemed out of place. One pale scientist, Dr. Allen, paced the room. A flustered, heavy-set Dr. Morgan barged in.

"Why the hell did you call the police?" Morgan's eyes flashed crimson red.

Allen backed away, nervously wiping beads of sweat from his brow.

"This is a disaster." Morgan glared at him. "No one's supposed to know about this." He grumbled under his breath. He should have seen this coming. He knew Martin had been up to something. Moving to a nearby desk, he opened a locked drawer and pulled out paper after paper. His face froze. He didn't want to believe Martin would really do it...but the diagrams in his hands said it all.

"Is that...?" Allen asked. The remaining color drained from his face. "But...can he really---?"

"You know exactly what he can do," said Morgan with rage in his eyes. Then he hesitated. "We have to call them."

Allen nervously shook his head.

"We have to tell them. It was our responsibility." Morgan slammed the drawer shut. "Damn it. I knew I should have gotten rid of the guy a long time ago."

"Maybe the police can still---" Allen said.

"No police! Don't you get it?" Morgan roared. "Get me the number. And keep your mouth shut. If this gets out..."

"But why would he---"

"Get me the number!"

Dr. Allen scurried out, narrowly missing two police officers entering the room. A gray-haired officer stepped forward.

"I'm Sargent Matthews. You reported a break-in?" His eyes surveyed the lab. His young zealous partner moved to his side.

Morgan moved aggressively toward them. "I'm afraid you were called by mistake, Gentlemen. Nothing's wrong here. Our security has already checked it out." He turned to usher them out, avoiding Matthews' piercing eyes.

Ignoring him, the younger officer split off and began wandering around the lab. "We were told someone stole something from the high security area of this building."

"It was a false alarm. Nothing's missing," said Morgan. He suddenly noticed photographs lying on the table. His eyes darted around the room. Someone was supposed to put those away.

The young officer noticed the photos lying on the table. His eyes narrowed. "Is that...?"

"Please don't touch those." Morgan darted over and gathered up the photos. "As I said before, our security's taken care of everything."

Morgan moved toward the door, keeping his eyes fixed on the officers. "We just do research here, Gentlemen. It's nothing that would interest you."

The officers stared at him.

"This is private property. So, unless you have a warrant, I'm going to ask you to leave," snapped Morgan.

The officers glanced at each other then walked out the door.

Outside, the morning mist was still lifting. The air was cool. Walking across the damp grass to their car, the officers stopped and looked back at the laboratory. They both knew the man was hiding something.

"What did you see in the photos?" asked Matthews.

"I didn't get a look at all of them, but what I saw was definitely the Shroud of Turin."

Matthews studied him. "The what?"

"The Shroud of Turin. Some believe it was the cloth Christ was buried in."

"Christ? As in Jesus Christ?"

"Yeah. They think it might have his image or blood on it."

"What do you mean it 'might' have?"

"I don't think they know for sure," said the young officer.

"How do you know all this?" Matthews asked.

"Twelve years of Catholic school."

Troubled, both men stared at the lab. The stone walls towered black against the gray sky.

A small candle flickered in the dimly lit room hidden deep inside the cathedral. Two men sat silently; their faces obscured in the shadows. One man donned a blood-red satin robe. A lavish ruby ring adorned his left hand. Across from him sat a man in black with polished manicured nails, a black and gold ring on his index finger.

The man in black shifted in his seat. "Did they say anything else?"

The man in red sat rigid as stone. "They found a note."

"They got a ransom note on a piece of cloth?"

"This isn't about money!" His red robes rustled. "The man's trying to destroy us."

"With a piece of cloth?"

"This isn't just any cloth!"

The man in black stood and paced the room. "Do we know for sure that the guy can really do this."

"We know exactly what he can do."

"But we have no proof that the Shroud is really---"

"What if it is?" The man in red fumed. He had no intention of giving up control over the empire he'd created. He had worked too hard. He liked the wealth. He liked the power. No renegade scientist was going to destroy it. He seethed as he turned to the man in black.

"I want you to send every man you've got to get this guy...before it's too late."

CHAPTER ONE

THIRTY YEARS LATER – NEW YORK CITY

Amy Michaels, a slender young woman with brown, sassy hair, dashed into the hectic New York newspaper office. She sighed as she saw the all-to-familiar scene. Throngs of serious-faced workers huddled over their computers, typing frantically, straining to meet unreasonable deadlines. The irritating florescent lights buzzed overhead.

She dropped down at her desk and wearily smiled over at Christine Adams, the forty-something, over-worked, mother-of-two working next to her. Christine's out-dated tailored suit was a bit disheveled. The roots of her bronze hair were long overdue for a touch-up.

"Morning Christine. Tonight's the school play, right?" Amy watched Christine's eyes light up. She knew her co-worker's greatest joy was to talk about her kids.

Christine nodded. "I'm trying to get this piece done so I can get out of here on time. Kari's the lead this time. Did I already tell you that?"

Amy grinned. Only twenty times a day for the past two months, she thought to herself.

Just then, Mr. Lawson stormed into the office. Amy cringed as she saw her boss aim right for them. Then Lawson, with his ruddy complexion and cheap brown toupee, hovered over Amy's disorganized desk and leered down at her laptop.

"Did you finish your piece on the world's ugliest dog yet? …Is this it?"

Amy quickly pulled her laptop toward her.

"No, Mr. Lawson. You asked Jackie to work on that story. You gave me five other assignments. I'm working on one of those right now."

He picked up a paper from her desk. "Well, what's this? Is this one done?"

"Not yet. You just gave me that assignment yesterday. I haven't proofed it yet," she said, reaching for the paper.

"I'm sure it's fine the way it is," he said gripping it even tighter. Amy would have had better luck pulling a chicken away from a fox.

"I need this now. I've got another idea I want one of you to work on." Lawson looked over at Christine who sheepishly swiveled back to her computer and started typing.

"I'll do it." Amy blurted out, trying to divert his attention away from Christine. "I'll get started on it right away." That is…after she figured out how to finish all the other absurd projects that he had dumped on her.

Tossing the paper back onto her desk, "Look in your email." Lawson turned and left. Amy laid her head on her desk.

"That man's gonna kill us," Christine said. "Amy, I don't know why you work at this stupid place. You're better than this. I had to take this job. I've got kids. But you've got bigger dreams than this."

Amy sat up straight and smiled. "Yeah. I'm gonna write a spectacular story that gets all of New York buzzing. A big publisher hears about it and offers me a huge advance to write my first best-selling novel, which of course, makes millions of dollars. Then I get my dad the best doctor in the world. He gets well. And we all live happily ever after."

Christine applauded.

Amy grinned and bowed. "Thank you. Thank you."

"Nice dream," Christine said.

"Now if I could just find the time to write that amazing story," whispered Amy under her breath.

"You're pretty much living at the hospital these days, aren't you," said Christine.

Amy glanced at a framed photograph on her desk; she and an older man are making faces at the camera.

"He's my dad." She'd be with him right now if it wasn't for this stupid job.

"Can't you take some time off, Amy? You look exhausted. You're not eating. You're not sleeping. You can't keep going like this."

Amy smiled. She hadn't quite figured out how to create money out of nothing.

"I was raised by a cop, remember? I can handle anything. Just finish your piece, Christine, so you can go. I'll take care of this one." Amy stuffed notes into her bag. More she'd be working on at home later tonight.

Amy's cell phone rang.

"Hello? ...Yes? ...What?! ...Oh my God! I'll be right there." Amy grabbed her coat. "My dad!"

Amy burst into her father's hospital room. Standing near the door, Dr. Mitchell grabbed her and pulled her aside. "He's okay. We got him back."

Amy pulled away and frantically darted to the bed nearest the door to find her father Frank Michaels, once a strong man, now weakened by time and illness.

Trying to hide her fear, Amy lovingly held her father's hand. "Hello, wonderful father of mine."

"Hello, light of my life." Frank strained to speak. "Don't you have any younger men to spend time with?"

"None as cute as you," she said.

"Well, at least they'd be less trouble."

Amy smiled. "Not in my experience."

She watched him squint, struggling to see. His eyes were tired and worn. His breathing was labored. His once quick, instinctive mind, sharpened from years of surviving on the streets as a cop in New York, was now fading. He'd had too much medication, too much chemotherapy.

Frank's area was surrounded by dozens of plants and pictures.

Near the window, lay a thin, older man, Mr. Evans. His area was gray, empty and sterile---an ironic reflection of the man himself. A half-closed curtain separated the two men. Even though Amy couldn't see his face, she knew the man was listening.

"Dad, what happened?" she whispered.

"Don't know. They didn't say much. I know that's not a good sign."

"Don't you worry about what they're saying. You and I will beat this. They don't know us."

Amy began pacing the room. She rearranged the many plants around his bed, doused them with cups of water, tucked in his blankets and then sat down beside him as if to protect him.

Fran smiled. "They're gonna have to zone us for agriculture soon,"

"They're to help you heal, Dad. They give off oxygen."

"We got enough oxygen here to reach Mars."

Amy smiled. She was determined to do whatever it took to get him well.

"How was work today, Honey?" He gazed at his daughter. "Did you save the world yet?"

"Hey, that's your job. I'm just gonna write about it when you do."

"Shut up out there!" Evans yelled from behind the curtain. "This ain't no damn party place."

"Sorry Mr. Evans." Amy lowered her voice.

Evans' foul moods and complaining had made her father's time in the hospital even more of a nightmare. She'd watched this temperamental man throw trays at the nurses and curse at any innocent orderly who dared to enter the room. She'd seen the otherwise compassionate and tolerant nurses argue in the halls over which of them had to deal with him.

"Amy, is the insurance company taking care of everything?" Frank asked.

"Don't worry, Dad. Everything's handled. We're fine." She quickly turned away before her eyes gave her away. He could always tell when she was lying.

"Where's that damn nurse?" Evans roared. "Nurse! Somebody get in here!"

11

Amy peeked around the curtain. "Can I get you something, Mr. Evans?"

"Leave me alone!" he yelled. "Mind your own damn business."

Just then, the plump and always friendly nurse Tess bustled in. Amy sighed with relief.

"Mr. Evans, please. Keep your voice down. What is it this time?" Tess caringly adjusted his pillows.

His eyes flared. "Where's my damn pills? I'm in a lotta pain here."

Retreating to a safer position at the foot of his bed, Tess examined his chart.

"You aren't due for your meds for another two hours---"

"I don't give a damn about what that stupid chart says!" His face raged bright purple. "I want those pills now!"

Tess backed away. "All right. All right. I'll see what I can do." She drew the curtain closed, then turned to Amy and pulled her aside.

"Honey, you must be exhausted. You've been in here every night."

Amy averted her eyes. What did she expect? This was her father, her best friend---and the only family she had.

"I know you said your mama died when you were just a baby, but isn't there anyone else who can help you?" Tess asked.

Amy shook her head. "It's just the two of us."

Tess gazed at the many pictures of Frank and Amy. "Don't you have any pictures of your mama?"

"I think it was too hard on him to keep them," Amy whispered.

Tess studied her. "You must look like her. You sure don't look like him."

"Yeah. I've been told that before," Amy said. She gazed at her father. She'd wondered if that had been hard on him...if he saw her mother every time he looked at her.

Hours later, Frank had finally fallen asleep. Amy brushed a lock of her father's hair off his face. Evans grumbled to himself.

Exhausted, Amy stood, picked up her bag, and turned toward the door. As she passed by a small mirror in the room, she caught a glimpse of herself. She didn't recognize the person she saw. Stress, fatigue, and worry had claimed her youthful appearance. She sighed, then took a deep breath, held her head up, and stepped out into the hallway.

Just outside the door, Dr. Mitchell was rushing by. Amy grabbed him.

"Excuse me, Dr. Mitchell. What's happening to my father? He seems to be getting worse."

"We're still running tests," he said. "You know, we're not sure how many more of these episodes he can handle. This is the third one this week."

"Well, don't give up on him! He's a cop. He's a tough guy." The resignation she heard in his voice scared her. Was she the only one fighting for her father, the only one believing he could get better?

Just then, Amy noticed a mysterious man with thick dark hair standing nearby. He had a tranquil strength about him. He was staring at her with the deepest eyes she'd ever seen. He smiled at her and nodded. Uncomfortable, Amy quickly turned back to the doctor.

"There's got to be something more you can do. "Aren't

there any new treatments we can try? Experimental drugs, herbs, shamans? Anything?"

"We're doing all we can." The doctor turned and walked away.

Glancing back down the hall, Amy noticed the mysterious man hadn't taken his eyes off her. There was something... strangely familiar about him. Realizing that she was staring at him, Amy pulled herself away. She slipped over to Tess at the nurse's desk.

"Did Jesse's mom make it here today?" Amy whispered discretely.

Tess shook her head. "Nobody to watch her other kids again."

"Poor Jesse." Amy glanced down the hall. The mysterious man was gone.

Amy shifted back to Tess. "Any word yet on when the work will be done on the children's wing so these little guys can be back with the other kids?"

Shaking her head, Tess said, "No, they're still behind schedule. It's a shame that we have to squeeze those three little angels into one room, but that's all we have right now. At least they have each other."

Tess leaned over to Amy and whispered, "Go on in. I know she feels better when you're in there."

Amy nodded, then slipped into a room where three young children lay sleeping in their beds. Various intravenous tubes and wires ran from their fragile bodies to nearby bottles and machines. There were parents sitting beside two of the children. Only one frail, four-year old little girl, Jesse, was alone.

Jesse opened her eyes, glanced up, and smiled weakly at Amy. The girl's skin was ashen white. Her eyes were sunken and weary. There were only scruffy tuffs of white hair where beautiful red curls use to be.

"How's beautiful princess Jesse today?" Amy smiled gently. She reached into her bag and pulled out a stuffed toy kitten. Amy fondly gazed at it. The cat was worn and faded from time and too many hugs. One button eye had long since disappeared. Tied around its neck was a pink ribbon with the name 'Mrs. Paws' handwritten on it.

"I know you miss your mommy," Amy whispered. "So, I brought you somebody special to sleep with." Amy offered the precious keepsake to her young friend. "This is Mrs. Paws, the best kitty in the whole world. She's been my best snuggle friend since I was little."

Grinning, Jesse pulled the stuffed kitten close and squeezed it. Her young smile both warmed and saddened Amy.

Tired and discouraged, Amy walked down the streets of New York. It was late. It was dark. People passed by - ordinary people with normal lives. She was too tired to notice them.

Suddenly a strange feeling came over her. Glancing over her shoulder, she noticed the mysterious man from the hospital walking not far behind her. She increased her pace. He increased his. She crossed the street. He crossed behind her. She wound amidst other people. The man still followed her.

Amy quickly slipped into a small cafe. Her heart pounding, she watched to see if he followed her. She peered through the window. There was no sign of him.

Suddenly, a waitress stepped up beside her. Amy jumped.

"Can I help you?" the waitress asked.

"Uh...no, thanks." Amy squirmed. "I'm just...um...I'm not staying."

Eyeing Amy suspiciously, the waitress walked away. Amy continued to watch the window. There was still no sign of the man. Her father had taught her to stay calm in the face of danger, not to let anyone sense fear in her. But she was beyond tired. She knew that was when people made foolish mistakes.

Moments later, the waitress returned and glared at her. With one eye on the impatient waitress, Amy opened her purse and fumbled around inside it.

"All right. All right. I'm leaving." Amy discretely pulled out a can of mace then ventured outside. There was no one in sight.

Amy walked slowly into her dark apartment, threw down her coat and bag, and slumped into a nearby chair. Alone, exhausted, and empty, she sat quietly in the dark for what seemed like hours. She had no energy to write tonight.

Then finally she wearily stood, opened the refrigerator, saw that there was nothing inside, and dragged herself to bed. As she curled up in bed, tears filled her eyes.

"God. It's me again. Please help my dad and all those little children. Please." As tears flowed down her cheek, she fell asleep.

CHAPTER TWO

The next day, a tired but determined Amy walked down the hallway of the hospital. Nurses and doctors rushed by in all directions. Amy stopped, leaned against the wall, and closed her eyes. She knew she needed to muster up all the strength and courage she could before she walked into her father's room again. She knew it was her unwavering tenacity that kept him fighting for his life.

She took a deep breath, straightened her shoulders, put on her bravest face, then continued down the hall. She paused for a moment to peek in on the children. As she peered through the doorway, chills ran up her spine. She gasped.

The mysterious man was sitting by Jesse. His powerful presence dwarfed the young child's frail little body. Amy watched as the man touched Jesse on the forehead. The small girl opened her eyes and looked at him.

Panicked, Amy pulled back. Her eyes searched the hallway. It was now eerily empty. Where were the doctors and nurses? Where were the parents? Why were these children all alone? She peered again through the door.

Jesse gazed up at the mysterious man. Then a calm look crossed her face. "Hi," Jesse whispered. "Was I sleeping?"

The man nodded.

"I dreamed I was really sick," she said.

The man held her hand. "As long as you know now that it was just a dream."

Jesse smiled and nodded.

Amy stiffened and braced to rush in when Tess strolled around the corner. Amy grabbed her.

"Tess, there's a man in there with Jesse. Is he supposed to be in there?"

"What man?

"There's a man in there with Jesse!"

Tess bolted into the children's room. There was no man in sight. All the children were asleep, except Jesse. The small girl looked up and smiled. There was a twinkle in her eye. A bewildered Amy could only stare at her.

Hours later, Amy sat quietly beside a sleeping Frank. Glad that, once again, medication had allowed her father to escape his pain for a while. She gently closed her laptop. Glancing at the monumental pile of mail and bills strewn at her feet, she sighed then gathered up all the papers and stuffed them into her purse. She stepped out into the hall, headed for home.

Suddenly, Amy heard the children squealing. Alarmed, she dashed down the hall. Reaching their room, Amy quickly pushed open their door. Her mouth dropped. All the children were giggling and jumping on their beds. Cords and feeding tubes lay haphazardly on the floor.

"Oh my God." Amy gasped. "What's going on?"

"She remembers who she is," said a voice behind her.

Amy spun around. It was the mysterious man. A charming, easy-going smile spread across his face.

"It's okay. It's just me," he said.

Amy pulled back, her eyes quickly evaluating her best escape route.

"I didn't mean to scare you," he said. "I forget how rampant fear is here."

"Here? What do you mean here? Who are you? What do you want?"

He smiled at her. Amy felt herself being drawn inside his deep, mysterious eyes. She forced herself to pull away. She looked wide-eyed at the children, then back at the stranger.

"Did you do something to that little girl?"

"I just helped her remember," he said.

"What? All those children have cancer. What did you do to them?"

He smiled as he glanced through the doorway at Jesse. "She helped them remember. Most children aren't attached to their movies. They're easier to reach."

Amy's head told her to bolt. Her body wouldn't move.

"Movies? What are you talking about?"

He sighed. "Y'know...as a child, you hear stories of magic and happily-ever-after. Then people take those away from you and convince you that struggle, hard work, and pain are what's real."

He gazed at the little girl. Amy saw both delight and sadness in his eyes.

"I just reminded her of the magic," he said.

She stared at the children in disbelief. Her head was spinning.

Curious hospital workers started to gather around the children's doorway. A large nurse, Maxine, barreled around the corner, pushed everyone aside, and barged into the children's room.

"Stop it!" she yelled. "Stop it all of you. You're sick. Lie down. Now!"

The man smiled at Jesse across the room. "Remember," he whispered.

The little girl beamed. A look of wisdom and understanding crossed her face. She nodded. Then she continued giggling and jumping on her bed.

Amy stared at them with bewilderment. "Will they be okay?"

"Hopefully. Adults can be pretty convincing." Then the mysterious man turned to Amy. "Would you like to go some place to talk?"

"What?" Amy stepped back.

Realizing her uneasiness, he added, "Some place with bright lights and plenty of people."

"Are you kidding me? I'm not going anywhere with you."

"There's no room for fear," he said. "If we're going to help your father---"

"My father? What does my father have to do with this?"

"You asked for help. I'm here to help."

"I didn't ask you for anything."

He smiled. "I can help you with your father. But you need to trust me."

"Trust you?" she blurted. "What do you mean trust you? I don't even know you."

He leaned in. "A moment ago, you were willing to try anything to help him."

There was something comforting about his voice. Amy was confused and suspicious but strangely drawn to him.

"Why should I believe you can help my father? The doctors don't even believe they can."

He paused and looked deep into her eyes. "For that very reason. The doctors don't believe they can help him. I know I can."

A shiver ran through Amy's body.

Amy sat at the restaurant clutching a cup of coffee. Wary yet mesmerized by this intriguing stranger sitting across from her, she watched him with guarded curiosity. Why did he feel so familiar? There was a sense of deep serenity about him. She sat in wonder as he enjoyed every morsel of food before him. He raised up each bite, admired it and placed it ever so delightfully in his mouth. Could he really be this excited about food? Or had it just been that long since he'd eaten? Compassion suddenly welled up in her. With all her attention focused on her father lately, she had forgotten that there were a lot of struggling people in the world who didn't even have a roof over their heads.

The waitress tossed the bill down on the table. Amy watched the mysterious man. He made no attempt to grab it. He seemed oblivious to its presence. She discretely opened her purse to assess her money. One lone, twenty-dollar bill stared back at her. She looked at the man, the bill, and then at the man.

"Why do I have the feeling you don't have the money to pay for this?" she finally asked.

"Why would I need money?"

She searched his eyes. "Are you homeless?"

He smiled and shook his head. "Anywhere I am, is home."

Amy rolled her eyes. Yeah, that's just what she needed... philosophy from the streets.

"Besides," he said. "You're the one with the pieces of paper, aren't you? Isn't that what those are for?"

"Pieces of paper? You're calling money pieces of paper?"

"Pieces of paper with pictures." Then under his breath, he whispered, "If people would realize that they'd be a lot happier."

"I work hard for those pieces of paper," she said.

"Why?"

Amy's mouth dropped. "Why? So I can feed myself and have a roof over my head. I'm responsible so I'm not a burden on society. That's the way life works."

"Is it?"

"What does that mean?"

There was a mischievous twinkle in his eyes. "Just curious to hear your beliefs about life."

"It looks like my beliefs are different than yours," she said with more than a touch of irritation in her voice.

"Apparently so." A broad grin crossed his face. He picked up a muffin, admired it, and stuffed it into his mouth.

Okay, forget about compassion for this guy. How could she have been so naïve? The guy probably told her he could help her just so he could get a free meal.

"Who are you?" Amy asked.

"Hmm. You need a name, don't you?" He glanced around the cafe.

"You can call me John."

"John what?"

"John." He smiled.

Silence. Why was he toying with her? What did he want? And what possessed her to sit here with this strange man? What was she thinking? If her father ever found out... With all her training as a cop's daughter? She knew better than to do something this stupid. She grabbed her purse and started to slide out of her seat.

"I can help you figure out how to heal your father." His voice was calm.

"Help me figure it out? I thought you knew how to help him."

"I do. You apparently don't. I'm here to teach you."

"You're going to teach me how to heal my dad of cancer?" Amy sneered.

"In a manner of speaking."

"And just how do you intend to do that?"

"You want basics, huh?" He looked out the window. "Okay. How about quantum physics."

"Quantum physics? That's basic to you?"

John continued to gaze out the window. Then he leaned into Amy and whispered. "What if I told you that all this around you is no more solid than those clouds out there? That it's all just energy."

"What?"

"Your scientists know now that there's nothing solid about matter." He lifted a glass of water and jiggled it. "You still believe that what you see is real. But it's no more solid or real than what you see in your dreams."

Amy stared at him. "I'm not sure how to relate to that." She surveyed the room. "It all looks pretty solid to me."

"The world looks flat to you too and you know that's not

the truth." He looked deeply into her eyes. "You wanted it to look real. It makes the movie more interesting." For a moment, his eyes filled with sadness. "But it's become too real for you. You've trapped yourselves in a world you've created. You've forgotten the truth."

Why was he staring at her that way? It was if he was searching her face for some sign of realization.

She backed away. "What are you talking about?"

He sighed. "Movies. ...Dreams. That's what this is. You're creating your very own three-dimensional production. But you've forgotten that." He looked intently into her eyes and whispered. "Do you know that when you're dreaming, everything in the dream feels real to you? You don't know you're dreaming until you wake up."

Amy was transfixed. Everything around her started to melt into a hazy blur.

"If you would only remember...like children. They know about pretending."

Amy shook herself out of her trance. "I don't understand," she snapped. "What does this have to do with anything ...with my father? And what happened to those children?"

His brow furled. "If you'd remember the truth, you'd be free. You'd be able to create anything you want. You'd actually enjoy life again." He paused and looked away. "And you'd understand what just happened with those children."

Amy hesitated. She studied his face. Who was he? Where did he come from? Then, as if he was reading her mind, John stopped.

"About thirty years ago, someone broke into a lab." He watched her. "Someone stole a small piece of cloth."

"Cloth?"

"This piece was special."

"Oh, I see." She smirked. "Special cloth. Like... Superman's cape?"

John smiled. "The scientists in this lab were running tests on the Shroud of Turin. You've heard of it?"

"The blanket they think Christ was wrapped in?"

He nodded. "They were running some experiments."

Amy watched this mysterious man.

"The people who stole the piece of Shroud did some experiments of their own." He continued eating. He seemed to be in no hurry to finish his strange story. Then finally he looked up. "Your scientists had just begun experimenting with cloning."

"Cloning? Thirty years ago?"

John smiled. "They don't tell you everything."

"And?"

"And ...you're looking at the result of one of those experiments."

Amy stared at him. "What? What are you saying? ...You were cloned? ...Off the Shroud?" Suddenly her eyes grew wide. "You're saying you're...you're Christ?!"

"I didn't say---" he started.

She pulled back.

He paused and gazed off into the distance. "Well. ...I guess some would see it that way."

"You're telling me you're Christ? ...The Almighty Son of God? Here in New York? ...And I'm supposed to believe that?" Her heart raced. Her blood pressure soared.

"Well, if---" he started.

She jumped up. "Look John...or whatever your name is. I'm leaving. You have a nice life. Stay away from me. And my father. I don't want to have to call..." She pulled her purse closer. "There are a lot of clinics in this city. I think you should go talk to someone."

She reached into her purse for the twenty-dollar bill and found...two twenties. She looked up. John smiled. Shocked, she dropped both twenties on the table and dashed out.

Tess glanced up and down the hospital hallways, then whispered to Amy. "Just don't stay in there too long. People are a little edgy around here right now."

Amy slipped into the children's room. Jesse and the other children were sitting up in their beds. Surprisingly, their faces were now rosy and vibrant. They almost seemed to be glowing. Jesse was dancing in bed with the toy cat. Shocked, Amy was speechless. Was this the same little girl?

"Princess Jesse?" Amy moved closer. "How are you?"

"Fine." Jesse smiled up at her. Then her smile fell. "Are you taking Mrs. Paws?"

"No, Honey. You get to keep her." Amy sat down next to her.

Jesse smiled and squeezed the cat. Amy peered at the stuffed animal. Was that her Mrs. Paws? The cat now had both eyes. It was still donning the same pink ribbon but seemed to be cleaner and ...even looked newer.

"Jesse, did somebody fix Mrs. Paws for you?"

"I did." The girl giggled proudly.

"You fixed her? How did you do that, Honey?"

"I was just dreaming before. Now she's better."

"What?"

Jesse smiled. "He told me. I was just dreaming."

"Who told you that?"

"The man.

Confused and bewildered, Amy could only stare at her. Smiling, the little girl reached over and patted Amy's hand.

"You forgot too, huh?"

Amy held her breath, as if she was about to hear a wise old soul share all the secrets of the universe.

With a twinkle in her eye, the little girl leaned in and whispered, "Remember fairy godmothers?"

Amy's eyes widened. "Did that man tell you he was a fairy godmother?"

Jesse giggled with her four-year old innocence. "No."

Just then Maxine barged in wrestling with a wheelchair. She charged toward the small girl.

"All right Jesse Marie. Let's go."

Amy's mind reeled. She needed more. She needed Jesse to stay.

Amy jumped up. "Where's she going?"

"That's hospital business," Maxine said in a voice that almost dared someone to challenge her.

Jesse screwed up her face. Then, still clutching the cat, she leapt out of bed and hopped into the wheelchair.

"Knock that off, Young Lady," Maxine snapped. "You're sick, remember."

As Jesse was wheeled out, she smiled back at Amy. Amy could only watch her leave.

CHAPTER THREE

Back at the office, a dazed Amy slowly typed at her computer. She stopped then turned to Christine.

"What do you think he did to those kids? Nothing, right? It was just a coincidence. The kids were already getting better, that's all." She turned and continued typing. Then she looked back at Christine.

"I mean, c'mon. Cloning? Get real. ...Why do I always attract the crazy ones?"

Christine opened her mouth to speak but---

"Never mind." Amy wasn't watching. "It's crazy. It doesn't even make sense." She continued typing, then paused and stared at Christine. "There was actually something about him though. He felt...I don't know... familiar...or something. I don't know how to explain it."

Christine stared at her.

"I'm just tired, right?" Amy searched Christine's eyes. "God, I'm starting to ramble like... Look what this place is doing to me."

Christine peered at Amy closely. "This guy actually told you he was Christ?"

"Well. No. He didn't say that exactly. But he said he was cloned...from the Shroud of Turin. How weird is that?"

Suddenly, Mr. Lawson towered over them. Amy jumped.

"Is this story done?" He squinted to read the screen on Amy's laptop.

"No. It's not done," Amy said as she quickly pulled away her laptop and turned away from him. Please God, tell her he didn't hear their conversation. Make him go away. She could kick herself. How did she not see him coming? How was he able to sneak up on them? If she could get down on her knees right now and pray that he'd go away without mentioning----

"Did I hear you say someone told you he was cloned?" Lawson's eyes were lit up.

Amy's heart sank. Thanks God. Couldn't you have just answered this one little insignificant prayer? Don't you know this man? Don't you know how he thinks? Amy paused. Her mind raced. What could she come up with to distract him? What could she say to twist around what he thought he heard her say?

"I was just talking about some homeless guy. It wasn't important." She placed her hand on top of her laptop. "I'm almost done with this story."

"No, I heard you say some guy told you he was cloned. Did you ask him how or where?"

"No." She winced. "He was just some homeless guy... crazy probably or on drugs."

"You didn't get his story?" Bits of spit flew from his mouth. "Some guy thinks he's cloned, and you don't find out if he's for real?"

"For real? He's not cloned. He's just---"

"I want this story." He'd already stopped listening.

"There's all kinds of angles here." Pacing, Lawson mumbled to himself. "Cloning. Yeah. That's a new one."

"But he says he's---"

"Get this guy's story."

"What? I don't even know where he is."

"Find him," he said.

"In New York?"

"Find him."

"But I have all these other---"

He towered adamantly over her. "Find him.

Amy stomped out of the building. With clenched jaw, she mumbled to herself. "I swear. One of these days..."

The air was chilly. The snow had melted but spring had yet to arrive. The frost-covered ground was still a muted brown. People rushed by clutching their coats.

Just then, Amy noticed a familiar form standing nearby. It was John. He was smiling at her. She cringed, turned, and quickly walked the other way.

John sprinted after her. "Where are you going? I've been waiting for you."

Oh God, she thought to herself. I thought I was just having a bad dream.

"You have been," he said as he followed her.

She continued to walk away from him.

"I thought I told you to leave me alone."

"Don't you need me for your article?"

"What?" She whipped around. "How did you---? Are you and my boss working on some scam?"

"No," he said. "You and I just have work to do. Do you want to grab a bite to eat?"

"No, I don't," she snapped. She turned and continued walking.

He followed. "Don't you have a story to write?"

Amy increased her pace. "Not if I couldn't find you."

"Ah, but I've found you. Aren't you even a little bit curious---"

Amy spun around. "Listen John. Or whatever your real name is. This paper will make you look like an idiot. This isn't the kind of publicity you want. Just let me tell my boss I couldn't find you and save both of us the time and the embarrassment. Please. Just go away."

John smiled...that irritating little smile that Amy found unsettling.

"Let's just walk a little," he said.

She ignored him and turned to leave.

"I guess I could go back and wait for you at your office," he said.

Amy halted. She looked nervously over her shoulder at the office building, then at John.

"I can't believe I have to do this." She mumbled under her breath. "I have to get a real job."

An irritated Amy marched defiantly down a path in the park as John strolled next to her. Amy, keeping her distance, glanced over at him. He still had that soothing energy, something about him that made her want to trust him. What was it? Why did he feel so...? It was a vague feeling, just on the edge of her awareness, like she'd known him from some other place or some other time. A peaceful feeling moved through her, a peace she'd never felt before. Shaking herself out of it, Amy stopped. She knew she shouldn't let her guard down...ever.

She glared at him. "Look. If I write this article, I want to know your real story...the truth, from the beginning. No weird stuff."

He smiled. "I will always tell you my truth."

"Your truth? No. I want THE truth."

"We can only tell the truth as we perceive it."

"Oh, great start," Amy muttered.

As they continued walking, Amy reached into her coat pocket and pulled out her phone. She started the recorder.

"Okay. So, who are you?"

"I told you."

"Cloned from the Shroud?"

"Yes."

Frustrated, she stopped the recorder. "How do I know you're really who you say you are?"

"How do you know you're really who you say you are?"

"What?" she asked. "What does that mean?"

"How do you know you're who you think you are?"

Amy glared at him. "I just know."

"Are you sure you're not just seeing a picture that everyone else has painted for you?"

"What are you talking about?"

John touched a tree as they passed by, love and admiration in his eyes. "Do you see yourself as mere flesh and blood? A body with a brain?"

"Well, science---"

"Science used to believe the earth was the center of the universe. Do you think they know everything now?" He shook his head. "These old beliefs keep you stuck in the movie."

"Again, with the movies." Amy looked up at the sky. "These are awfully profound words coming from the Son of God. Life is a movie and I'm making the whole thing up. If that's true...then I deserve an Academy Award for this one."

He smiled. They made eye contact. Amy squirmed then turned on the recorder. How could she find out who he really was? Maybe if he let something slip about his past.

"Okay. If you were cloned thirty years ago, as you claim, where have you been all this time? Where were you as a child?"

"It doesn't matter where I've been."

Amy turned off the recorder. She was getting nowhere with this guy.

"The past isn't important," he said as he shook his head. "People drag their past around with them and think that's who they are." He looked intently into her eyes. "It doesn't matter what you've done or where you've been. What's important is who you choose to be NOW."

As they continued walking, Amy noticed his continuous fascination with the world around him. As they passed by shrubs or trees or even benches, he would touch each one and smile. It was as if he was...in love with everything. And yet, she sensed something else in him...sadness, loneliness. There was a look, deep in his eyes. She recognized that look. She saw it in her own eyes. What would make him so sad? Was it something from his past? Was he hiding something?

They turned a corner to find an enormous, beautiful fountain with a statue of an angel in the center, the famous

Bethesda Fountain. John stood and admired its beauty. Amy once again turned on the recorder.

"If you're really who you say you are, why don't you go to the Vatican or the President or somebody important?"

"They think they're happy with their movies," he said. "They have wealth and power and fame. They think they already know all the answers."

Nearby, an old man was selling hot dogs from a cart. A homeless man searched through a trashcan. A man and woman argued and angrily stormed away from each other. John gazed at them. For a moment, deep compassion emanated from his eyes.

Then John walked over to the cart and admired the hot dogs. He turned and smiled at Amy. He just stood there. And stood there. And stood there. …Bewildered, Amy shrugged. Then realizing what he wanted, she grunted and stomped over to pay for his hot dog.

"Then there are those who aren't happy with their movies." John winked at her. She diverted her eyes.

He overloaded his new treat with every condiment available. Then he held up the hotdog like a well-earned trophy, admired his work of art, and passionately consumed it.

Still perplexed by this strange man, Amy turned on the recorder.

"So why don't you teach a workshop or speak in Central Park or something? Gather the masses."

"Change is better when it starts inside. Trying to change the masses from the outside just creates riots and wars." He gazed off in the distance. "The crowds will show up sooner or later anyway. They always do." He looked at Amy. "But crowds can get ugly...and people tend to hear what they want to hear. You'll find that out soon enough."

A shiver ran up Amy's spine.

As they walked, John noticed a homeless woman sitting on a nearby bench. The woman pulled out a stale piece of bread from a small brown paper bag and nibbled on it. She tossed the empty bag aside.

John quietly walked over to the woman and sat down. He picked up the woman's tattered paper bag. Then he opened it, looked inside, smiled, and handed it back to her. He held the woman's hand as they talked. Amy couldn't take her eyes off this perplexing man. John then stood and returned to Amy.

"What?" she asked. "You need more food?"

John chuckled, then sat down on a nearby weathered bench. Still cautious, Amy stood off to the side.

"So, what are you doing here?" she asked.

John glanced up at a dogwood tree and watched as flowers began appearing on the tree.

"People have forgotten the universe is a creative playground," he said. "They have the ability to create love and joy and happiness. They have free will."

Amy could've sworn she caught a glimmer of joy in his eyes. She followed his gaze. Her body suddenly jolted. There it was---a fully blossomed tree. The other trees had no blossoms at all. Did that tree have flowers before? Did she just not notice that? Had she been so focused on John she just hadn't been paying attention? Not sure what she was seeing, Amy glanced nervously at John, then stared at the blossomed tree.

"When people dream," he said, "they remember how to create by thought. They imagine themselves somewhere and they're there. They imagine flying and they fly. There are no limits."

Just then a flock of birds soared by.

"But then they imagine themselves here again...in what they think is the 'real' world. Where they think life is pain, struggle, illness, and death. They've turned their dreams into nightmares."

Catching a hint of sadness in his voice, Amy cautiously sat down at the far side of the bench. She had a sense he was no longer just talking to her. What did this man need to say...and to whom?

He sighed as he watched people on bikes angrily yell and curse at the people in their way.

"People imagine that life is hard, so it's become that for them," he said sadly. "They imagine that disease, crime, and hatred are real, so they continue to create that. They've forgotten who they are. They've forgotten the magic."

Gazing around at more blossoming trees, John took a deep breath, then smiled.

"Deep inside, they all remember a time when life was easy...a beautiful garden. And they long for that easy life again." He gazed up at the sky. "But they imagine that easy place, that 'heaven' to be somewhere else...sometime in the future. They don't imagine heaven to be here and now, so they don't experience it here and now." He looked into Amy's eyes.

"People started believing that humans were bad and shameful, no longer deserving of that beautiful garden. Then they stopped believing in the garden entirely." He shook his head. "Fear imagines fear. Love imagines love. People now fear more than they love."

Amy watched as the homeless woman sitting on the

bench nearby shared a small piece of her bread with a scruffy squirrel.

"So, you really believe we have free will to create any life, any 'movie' we want?" Amy paused. "Why would someone choose to be poor?"

Just then, a harried man in a business suit rushed by them. He was yelling into his phone. His face was tense. He seemed unaware of anything around him.

John looked at Amy. "You think money's always better?"

The businessman's eyes were focused straight ahead. His mind was somewhere else. He was quickly gone.

"Just because we don't understand why someone would choose a certain life," John said, "It doesn't mean that they didn't choose it."

Amy had lost herself in his deep gaze. She could feel the warm empathy radiating from him. She almost felt sorry for him. How lonely it must be for him to feel he had important things to say, but no one was listening.

Amy realized that a crowd of homeless people had gathered around the woman with the small brown bag. The woman was pulling large chunks of bread out of the bag for each of them. Oddly, the bag now seemed to hold an endless supply of bread inside.

John smiled. "But these are my beliefs. Everyone's free to believe and create any movie they want."

Amy couldn't take her eyes off the crowd. Was that the same bag? Amy watched as piece after piece of bread was pulled out. Shaken, Amy stared at John. She switched off the recorder and crammed it back into her pocket. She'd had enough.

John stood. "So, shall we go see your father now?"

"What? No!" Amy jumped up. "No offense. My boss

can make me write a story, but that's it. My father is off limits to you."

John looked at the ground and shook his head.

"Don't you have some place else to go?" she asked. "Some lepers to heal or something?"

"No. I have work to do with you."

"Well, you can't go with me." Amy backed further away. "I'm sure I have enough from you. Movies, dreams, I think I've got it. So, thank you. Good luck. Goodbye."

As she turned to leave, she suddenly felt an uneasy shiver run through her entire body. An oppressive and thick energy now hung in the air. What was happening? It was eerie...and unsettling. In the distance, she thought she saw a man in black standing in the shadows. Amy looked at John, then back at the shadows. There was no one there. Amy shuddered. She backed away, then turned, and bolted off.

CHAPTER FOUR

Amy stepped out of the hospital elevator...and into a strangely barren hallway. Where was everyone? There was no one...not even a nurse in sight. Concerned, Amy quietly made her way to the children's room and slipped in. She gasped. All the beds were empty!

"Oh my God. What's going on?" Her breathing quickened. Her eyes searched the room. Was she in the right room? Yes, there were the children's drawings on the wall.

Tess suddenly stepped into the room behind her. Amy jumped.

"Tess! Where are the kids? What's happened? Did they move them? Where's Jesse?"

"They went home," Tess whispered.

"Home? What?! Why?"

"Nothing's wrong with them." Tess smiled nervously.

"What are you saying?" Amy reeled. She gazed around the children's room.

"The cancer disappeared," said Tess.

"Completely?" Amy gasped. "All of them? How? The chemo...radiation?"

"With all of 'em at the same time?" Tess shook her head.

"Twenty years I've been here. Never seen anything like this. Overnight. Poof! Cancer's gone. It's sure shaking this place up." Then she smiled. "Isn't it great though? All those little angels got to go home."

"This is a…a miracle! Why didn't someone announce this? Why wasn't this blasted all over the news or social media…or something?"

"Shush, Amy. You can't say anything. They don't want the publicity." Tess nervously glanced toward the door. "That's why they sent them all home so quickly. A lot of strange things have been happening around here. We're not supposed to talk about it."

"But if this really happened---"

"Amy, you can't say anything." Tess was visibly shaking.

"But won't people find out? Won't the parents say something?"

"None of the parents know what happened to the other kids," Tess whispered. "They only know their own child got better. They think the other kids were moved back to the other wing."

"But---"

Tess grabbed Amy's arm. " Please, Amy. You can't tell anyone. I can't lose my job over a strange scandal like this. Promise me."

Amy staggered back through the hallway toward her father's room. Tomorrow she would go to each and every doctor and find out what they knew about these children. And if they wouldn't tell her, she'd track down every child and ask them. Jesse would tell her. Jesse always told her the truth.

...And if the doctors could heal those children, why weren't they healing her father?

Amy stopped. What if Jesse told her that man did this? ...Well, she would just have to explain to the child that she was mistaken, that it wasn't possible. There had to be another answer.

Suddenly a loud alarm rang through the hallways. Doctors and nurses quickly appeared. They pushed past her and dashed into the room near her. An elderly woman was having a heart attack. The frightened patient in the nearby bed watched helplessly. There was no way for the roommate to get away from this disturbing scene.

Distressed, Amy watched as the doctors worked relentlessly on the woman for what seemed to be forever. But they were unable to revive her. They finally pulled the sheet over her. Discouraged, one by one, they left the room. Two orderlies wheeled in a gurney to remove the woman's body.

Shaken by what she had just seen and concerned that she may have just witnessed her father's future, Amy staggered down the hallway. She finally turned and entered her father's room. Maxine stood over Frank's empty bed. Fear suddenly filled Amy's eyes.

"Your father's having his treatment," said Maxine.

"Now? But it's so late."

"He wasn't up for it earlier," said the gruff Maxine. "He had a bad day."

Amy slumped down onto Frank's bed.

"They're going to have him in there for quite a while," Maxine grumbled. "And then they're going to want him to rest. You should just go home. You can see him tomorrow." She walked out.

Discouraged, Amy sat in silence.

All of a sudden, she was aware that there were people talking in low voices behind the curtain. Realizing that Evans hadn't been yelling at her, she cautiously peered around the curtain. She gasped. John stood holding Evans' hand. A tear ran down the old man's face.

"You'll see her again, I promise," John whispered. "She's still here for you."

Evans looked hopefully into John's eyes then he quietly gazed up at the ceiling. Amy felt a powerful wave of kindness and compassion radiating from John. Speechless, she couldn't take her eyes off him.

John gently squeezed the old man's hand, rose, smiled at Amy, then moved by her and stepped out into the hallway. Dumbfounded, Amy followed him.

"What are you doing in here? What did you do to that old man?"

John continued walking. "He's had a rough time. He's lonely."

"I'm not surprised, He's not a real friendly guy. He sure doesn't like it when I'm here."

"Jealousy is tough." John stopped and searched Amy's eyes. "His wife died three years ago. He has no family."

Silence. Ashamed, Amy looked away.

"Feeling sorry for people just keeps them stuck. It's better to see them as powerful and able to create a better life." John turned and continued down the hallway.

Amy rushed after him. "Did you bother my father?"

John continued walking. "So, he raised you all alone?"

"What? My father?" She grabbed John's arm, but he kept walking. "Yes, he did. How do you know that? What did you do?!"

"So much guilt and blame inside. That's what's eating him up."

"Guilt? My father?" She quickly let go of his arm. "You don't know what you're talking about. He's a great man."

"He's hard on himself."

"He's had a hard life." Amy snapped. "He had to be mother and father for me. He worked hard. And his job..." She took a deep breath, trying to control her emotions. Then she turned away and grumbled under her breath. "Why am I even telling you?"

John stopped and stared at her.

"Being a cop was tough," Amy said defiantly. "He worked long hours. But he was always there for me." She looked away. Angry tears filled her eyes. "He's my best friend. I can't bear the thought of losing..."

She choked up as they entered the elevator. The elevator started descending. Amy stared at the floor and tried to regain her composure as she wiped away tears.

John looked at her. "Do you mind if we make a stop?"

"What? Yes, I do mind. Bad things happen around you. I want to go home."

The doors opened onto a cold, isolated floor. Frustrated, Amy watched John walk out and down the hallway then turn into a room. The elevator doors closed. Amy just stood there...and stood there. The air was still. She pushed the up button. The elevator didn't move. She pushed it again. It didn't move.

Finally, apprehensively she opened the doors and stepped out. The quiet was unsettling. Amy crept down the hallway to see where John had gone. With every hesitant step, she wondered if she was going to live to regret her decision. Yet something kept pulling her on. There'd be no one near to hear her scream. And yet there she was, still inching forward. Her heart pounded as she neared the door where John disappeared. Her breathing quickened. She peered around the doorway to find...the morgue.

John stood motionless over a covered body. He pulled back the sheet. It was the woman who had the heart attack. Amy gasped. Her face turned white. Her body shook.

John took the woman's hand and focused intently on her. "Come back, Emma. Your daughter needs you." His voice was strong and commanding. "Come back." Silence. "Now."

The woman slowly opened her eyes.

Amy silently screamed. "Oh my God! Oh my God! Oh my God! This can't be happening!"

Horrified, Amy spun around and raced back to the elevator. The doors were closed. She frantically hit the elevator call button on the wall.

"I didn't listen to my dad. Should've listened to my dad," she ranted. "He told me Amy don't do stupid things. This is New York. There are crazy people out here." She pounded on the call button over and over. "God, just get me out of this and I promise I'll never do it again."

Meanwhile, John helped the woman to her feet. The woman was pale and disoriented. Sheet and hospital gown entangled around her body; the woman shuffled beside John out into the hallway.

Amy looked down the hallway to see them headed right for her. Terrified, she pounded on the elevator button again and again.

"Wake up Amy!" she screamed inside. "You're having a really bad dream."

The elevator doors slowly opened. Amy rushed in and

punched the close button. The doors wouldn't close. She hit the button again and again. The doors wouldn't move.

"What's happening?" she cried.

John appeared with the woman and gently guided her into the elevator. Amy pulled as far away from them as she could. The doors closed. Then a quick jolt as the elevator started to ascend. There was a deafening stillness. Amy could hear the blood pounding in her ears. The old woman stared at John.

The elevator jerked to a stop. The doors opened. John calmly coaxed the woman out. He watched as she slowly walked back to her room. Paralyzed with fear, Amy pressed flat against the back wall of the elevator. The doors closed. Amy's eyes were wide with terror. John stepped toward her. Amy recoiled. Shaking his head, John moved away from her and leaned against the far side of the elevator.

He sighed. "I see we still have a lot of work to do."

Trembling, her sense of reality dashed to pieces, Amy could barely speak. "Who are you? Are you the devil?"

"Why is it whenever people don't understand something," John said, "They automatically think it's evil or something to be afraid of?"

Amy was still in shock.

"You'd think that after all this time people would've outgrown the concept of evil. Why do you still believe in it?" he asked.

"What?" Amy stammered. "We...we believe in it because we see it all around us."

"No. You see it all around you because you still believe in it...so you continue to create it." He waited for her to regain her composure, but she continued to watch him in shock.

"As long as you're afraid, we can't move forward," he said.

"This can't be happening," she said still shaking. "I...I can't handle this."

"I wouldn't be here if you weren't ready for this."

The elevator stopped. The doors flew open. Amy bolted out. She ran down the empty hallway.

That night, trembling and pale, Amy huddled on her bed. All the lights were on. Crosses of every size lay in a tight circle around her. She had been clutching her knees to her chest so tightly that she could no longer feel her legs. Quivering, she stared at her phone lying nearby.

Who could she call – 911? ...And say what?

Christine? ...It's after midnight.

She had no one to call. No one to help her make sense of this nightmare. Amy didn't close her eyes that night.

CHAPTER FIVE

The next morning, Amy anxiously peered out from the hospital elevator. There was no one nearby. She cautiously stepped out into the hallway, then her heartbeat quickened. At the other end of the hall, the woman who had the heart attack sat in a wheelchair. She was surrounded by a swarm of doctors. Amy inconspicuously headed the other way and quickly slipped into her father's room.

Frank's room was eerily still. He was smaller and weaker than Amy had ever seen him as he lay sleeping, still struggling to breathe.

"Dad?" Amy whispered. "Dad, can you hear me? I need you. The world's gone crazy. Nothing's making sense anymore. Please talk to me."

Eyes closed; Frank lay motionless.

Dr. Mitchell walked in. His face was somber. His eyes, grave and foreboding. Dread washed over Amy. She knew why he was there. She wished he would just turn around and walk out. Why couldn't the world just leave them alone? Let her figure out how to handle this bad dream. She just needed more time.

The doctor motioned her aside.

"I'm afraid your father's tests aren't good." He paused. "I don't think there's much more we can do for him. You may have a very difficult decision to make soon."

Amy pulled away. Her head throbbed. Everything went dark as tears stung her eyes. The doctor, unsure what to say, withdrew from the room. Amy collapsed and laid her head on her father's hand.

"He's wrong Dad. You wouldn't leave me. Please don't leave me. I need you. Give me more time. I'll find a way. Please hold on." She whispered, "God, please help him."

Tormented. Distraught. Amy moved alone down the hospital hallway. She stopped and stared into the children's room. It was quiet...and empty. What miracle saved them? Where are they now? She glanced down the hall to see doctors still fussing over the old woman in the wheelchair. What was happening? Did she really see what she thought she saw? Amy stood in silence.

John sat in the park talking with the same group of homeless that were there before. Their eyes appeared to dance as they listened to him. The wrinkles on their tired faces were relaxed, softer. They seemed younger...and happier.

Surrounding their bench, thick, emerald-green grass. The trees nearby were heavy with white blossoms. People passed by, so lost in their own busy worlds they didn't even notice the lush green oasis surrounded by a brown, barren wasteland.

John looked up. Amy was standing across the way, watching him with tears in her eyes. Desperation and determination showed on her face.

John slowly rose. The crowd squeezed around him. Struggling to pull away, he broke free and moved toward Amy. The crowd started to follow. He calmly stopped them.

Amy warily stood her ground.

John and a shaken Amy crossed the street and walked along the sidewalk. People shoved by, darting in and out of stores and restaurants. John glanced at Amy but remained quiet. After a long tortuous silence, Amy finally turned to him.

"What happened to that woman? ...Did they make a mistake? Was she not really dead?"

John gently smiled. "That's closer to the truth than you know."

Amy stopped. "What happened? What did you do?"

He stopped and studied her. "I called her back."

"You called her back? How did you...? What does that mean? You called her back?"

John was silent.

"Do you have a right to do that? What if it was her time to go? What if she was better off where she was?"

"I wanted her back. I called her back. It's my movie. I can do whatever I want."

Amy reeled. "Whoa. Your movie? I thought you said it was my movie?"

"That's right. I did."

"Well, how can it be both your movie and mine?"

"There are an infinite number of movies." He continued walking.

Amy whispered, "Dad forgive me." She hurried to catch up with John. "I would sell my soul to save my father."

A look of compassion crossed John's face. He stopped in front of a store with televisions on display in the window. Each set was on a different show. He pointed to one.

"Look. That's one of your favorite actors, right?"

"A woman comes back from the dead, and you want to watch TV?" Amy had no time for this, not even to ask why he knew that.

They watched a few moments as the actor died in the movie. Silence. John looked at Amy with question in his eyes. Then he pointed to another set.

"Wait! There he is again! But I just watched him die. How did he do that?"

Amy stared in disbelief. "You're not serious, right?"

John stared at her.

Amy was dumbfounded. "They're just movies. He's acting. He didn't really die. ...You know that, right?"

"Yes, I do. Do you?"

"What are you telling me? That people don't really die? That it's all pretend like in the movies?"

He smiled.

"But...why do we go through all the pain and suffering of death if it isn't real?" she asked.

"Because you believe it's real...and that it's inevitable."

"It's not?"

"Death's not a real thing. It's an illusion. Like everything else." His voice was strong and passionate.

Amy looked bewildered. She wanted to understand. And she desperately wanted to believe him. But nothing in her life had prepared her for this.

John focused on her. "Your spiritual teachers have told you that you're eternal, right? When do you think eternal life begins? After you die? Eternal life has no beginning... and no end. Eternal is now and always."

He saw that Amy was still struggling. "You've just done the death scenes so many times, you've forgotten you don't have to end your movies that way."

They continued walking in silence.

Amy suddenly turned to him, her eyes flashing. "A friend died two years ago. If death isn't real, where is she?"

"She's still around you...watching in the wings, so to speak. You just don't believe you can see her because you believe she isn't physical. But in a sense, neither are you. Remember? There's nothing solid about matter. Everything is energy...energy and consciousness."

Amy stopped and searched John's eyes. "Can you see my mother?"

John paused, then walked to a small food stand nearby and ordered something to drink. Bewildered, Amy followed him, fumbled around in her purse for money, then paid. They stood in silence.

John pulled a large ice cube out of his drink. "This ice cube looks solid to you." He dropped the ice cube back into his drink and it instantly melted. "You think it's gone, but it's still there. Everything's still there. Your body is just energy. It's your thoughts that make it appear real. Just like in your dreams. You can imagine it taking any form you want."

"People are going to have a hard time believing this," Amy said.

"Then they're going to continue to experience pain and sorrow when they think they've lost someone."

Amy paused at the door of her apartment. John stood nearby.

Amy stared at him. "You know I would do anything to save my dad. But if you hurt me and I can't be there for him, I'll..." She clenched her jaw. "Be very, very angry."

Compassion in his eyes, John smiled at her as they entered. Amy tossed her coat down. Clutching her purse, she had a firm grasp on the can of mace inside. Keeping her eyes on John, she moved through her apartment turning on all the lights. She cringed as she realized her clothes lay scattered on the floor. Shoes were in disarray under and around the sofa. The sink was a mountain of empty dishes and soda cans. As she tripped over the chaos, Amy watched John grin. She jeered at him.

"I've had more important things to do," she said.

"People always have more important things to do," he said.

She backed her way to the refrigerator and opened the door. It was empty except for a few cans of soda.

"I don't have any food, but I can give you something to drink."

"Really?" he said. "I was actually looking forward to food."

"I bet you were." She pulled out one can and tossed it to him. Then she sat down across the room and stared at him. There was an unbearable silence. Anticipation, hope, skepticism...and fear all hung in the air.

Then frustrated, she said, "If you can really help my dad, please do it. ...Now."

"If you want to help him, remember who you are."

"That's it?"

"That's a lot," he said.

"I need more."

"Okay." He pondered as he looked around the room. "Remember everything is energy. Your thoughts direct that energy. Pay attention to your thoughts. See your father healthy and whole."

Amy stared at him.

"You just have to believe it's possible," he said.

Amy rolled her eyes. "So if I have faith, I can move mountains."

"Faith isn't just hope, it's knowing. When you KNOW what all this really is...you'll know you can move mountains... or walk on water...or change water to wine."

Amy glared at him. "Yeah, well great. That's a nice philosophy. But it doesn't work in the real world. I've tried that positive thinking. And my dad still has cancer. I work too hard. And I'm still broke. I can't even afford to keep food in this place." Fear and frustration in her voice, she was losing what strength and hope she once had.

He sighed as he looked around, then stood. Amy jumped up and pulled back.

John moved to the refrigerator. "Are you sure you don't want something to eat? An apple maybe?"

He opened the refrigerator. Amy gasped as she saw a refrigerator full of food. Her knees went weak. She collapsed onto the chair.

John grabbed an apple, closed the door, returned to his chair and sat down. Amy, keeping her distance, got up and staggered to the fridge. She opened it to find---it was empty.

"What just happened? Where did it all go?"

John smiled. "Now you wouldn't learn anything if I did it all for you, would you?"

"Oh, I don't like the sound of this." Exasperated, she closed the door. How was she going to understand what was real if it all kept disappearing?

"It's easy. What do you see in your refrigerator?"

Amy stared at him. "Nothing."

"Really? Okay then, open the door."

She opened the door to find an empty fridge.

"Huh." He smiled. "Very good."

She closed the door again.

"What do you see in there now?" he asked.

"Still empty," she said annoyed.

"Well. Let's see."

Again, she opened it. Again, it was empty.

"Why do we keep doing this?" she snapped.

"You tell me. You're the one who keeps saying it's empty."

"I keep saying that because that's what I see."

"Pay attention, Amy. This is very important. It's the other way around. You keep seeing an empty refrigerator because that's what you think and say."

Amy rolled her eyes. "Well, what do you think is in there?"

John paused. "Hmm. Let's see. I see chocolate cream pie, pudding, and... Oh, let's just fill it up."

Amy stared at him.

"Well?" he asked. "Aren't you going to open it?"

"I'm afraid to."

"That's part of the problem."

She opened the refrigerator to find it over-flowing with food.

"You'll find the pie and pudding on the top shelf," he said.

Amy stared at all the food. "I don't believe this."

"That's the other problem. Now it's your turn."

"No! Keep it in there, please. I need food and I obviously can't do what you do."

"Of course you can. You can do anything I can do. There's no difference between you and me...between anyone and me. I just know who I am. And you've forgotten." John looked deep into her eyes. "Believing you are powerless benefits no one."

The clock in Amy's apartment read 3:00 am. Glazed eyes, struggling to stay awake, Amy slouched over her computer working on a story. She didn't know what was real anymore... but she needed a paycheck until she could figure it out. She paused, pondered, then punched away at the keys.

CHAPTER SIX

The hospital was quiet. Frank lay motionless in bed. Amy sat by his side. She wondered if she was losing her mind. She wanted to believe it all. Something deep inside felt like it was all possible – that there was something more to reality. She remembered feeling as a child that people had it all wrong, that there was more to life than what the world was showing her. And now she saw the amazing things John was able to do. Maybe he was telling the truth?

But then her rational mind, the part that was raised by a down-to-earth cop and loving father told her otherwise.

She paused. She had to know.

She stared at her father as she considered what she was about to do. She looked around the room. Evans was sleeping behind the curtain. There was no one else in sight. Amy took her father's hand. Closed her eyes. Concentrated.

"Heal Dad. ...Please heal," she whispered.

Minutes ticked away. She heard the muffled sounds of traffic outside the window and the shuffling sound of footsteps in the hall as people passed by. More minutes ticked away. Amy could feel her own heartbeat. Even though it had only been minutes, it felt like forever. Taking a deep breath, Amy opened her eyes. Still unconscious, Frank struggled to breathe. Amy's heart sank.

The small diner was hectic that night but Amy, slumped in a booth by the window, didn't notice. The menu sat untouched in front of her. Amy slowly glanced around, then discreetly picked up a spoon and focused on it.

"Bend. ...Bend. Damn it. Bend."

A waitress suddenly stood over her. "Can I get you something to drink?"

Amy quickly dropped the spoon. "Um...just water right now. Thanks." Well, it was clear the waitress thought she was crazy. Amy guessed it wouldn't be long before everyone else would feel the same way. ...Although, she wasn't sure anymore if she cared.

Moments later, the waitress appeared with a glass of water then walked away. Amy stared at it. She glanced around again to see if anyone was watching. She discretely picked up the glass, then closed her eyes and concentrated.

"Wine. ...Be wine."

Silence. She stared at the water. It was still water. Amy slammed down the glass. Water splashed out everywhere.

Suddenly John stood over her.

She jumped. "Jesus Christ! Stop doing that!" Her heart was pounding. "My God. Don't you ever make a normal entrance?"

He smiled.

Amy wiped up water and organized her place setting. She watched as John sat, raised an eyebrow at her water and grinned.

60

"What are you doing here?" She paused, then slid her glass over to him. "Here. Do something. Turn it to wine or something."

"Why? You don't drink."

"I just need to see if..." She hesitated, then looked away.

"What's this about?" John studied her face.

Amy shook her head. "Nothing. Never mind."

The waitress hovered over her. "Are you ready to order?"

Amy turned away.

John opened the menu and pointed. "We'll have two of these."

The waitress sauntered away. Amy stared out the window.

"If you can really help my dad, why aren't you doing it?"

"Is something bothering you?"

"Yeah, something's bothering me," she said, whipping around and looking into his eyes. "I don't know what's going on. I just don't know what's real anymore. I could be dreaming all of this."

John smiled. "Exactly."

She scowled, then glared at him. "Look. My boss wants a story about you, but I don't want to give it to him. I never did find out what happened to those children. My dad's getting worse every day. And that woman...well, maybe she wasn't really dead in the first place."

John's smile fell.

"And the food?" he asked.

Amy squirmed and looked down. "I don't know. Maybe you're just a really good hypnotist. Maybe I just imagined it all."

"Well, you're right about that. You are imagining it all. And you have been hypnotized into believing something's real when it's not. ...But not by me."

Silence.

"You already wrote the story?" he asked.

"Yeah. But I told you. I'm not going to submit it."

"Did you use your real name?"

"Yes," she said.

"First and last?"

Amy stared at him. "Is there a problem? Is there something you're not telling me?"

"The others learned not to use their last names."

"Others? What others?"

"Fear still creates fear though." He gazed off in the distance.

His strange questions and the concern in his voice made her squirm. Was something terrible about to happen?

Their food arrived.

John's empty plates were scattered across the table. Amy's plate sat untouched. The waitress set the bill on the table. Sighing, Amy reached for it. John grabbed her hand. He patted his shirt pocket and pulled out a twenty-dollar bill.

"Where did you get that? " Amy whispered nervously.

John laughed. "He heals the sick and raises people from the dead but can't create paper with pictures?"

She squirmed and looked anxiously around the diner. "Well...that's not enough anyway."

John again reached into his pocket and this time produced a one-hundred-dollar bill.

"That better not be counterfeit." Her mind suddenly conjured up images of the entire New York police department barging in and dragging them away. On top of everything else, how would she explain that to her father?

"Oh ye of little faith," he said as he laid the money on the table.

"Are you going to leave all of that for her?"

"Why not? There's more where that came from."

As they walked outside, a sense of dread washed over Amy again. The air felt heavy and foreboding. Uneasy, she looked around, but saw nothing unusual. Still, something didn't feel right. Her body felt tight.

Amy hadn't noticed a man in black across the street, blending into the dark. The man's eyes were fixed on them. His black and gold ring caught the light.

John turned to Amy. "How about going to a movie?"

"A movie? What?" she stammered. "Now?"

"You want to help your father?" John had already started walking. Amy could see any protest from her would be futile.

What was he up to? Had John felt something too? If so, why didn't he say something?

"We're going to a real movie?" she asked, as she raced to catch up with him.

"You think there's a difference?"

The man in black watched them walk away. Then he crossed the street and entered the diner. He walked by their table and, with a gloved hand, grabbed John's glass and slipped it into his coat pocket.

Amy was numb as she sat in the theater staring at the movie screen. John's attention wandered around the theater.

"Amy?" he whispered.

Amy didn't notice he was speaking to her.

"Amy?"

"What?"

"Do you think those are real people up there on the screen?"

"What? Of course, those are real people. I can see them."

"But are those the real, actual people you're seeing?"

"Of course not," she said. "They're pictures of the real people."

"What you're seeing are tiny lights blinking on and off on a flat, two-dimensional screen. The lights make it appear that there are people there. But it's still just lights blinking off and on."

Amy stared at him. "Great. So now you're telling me that I don't really exist. I'm just a bunch of lights blinking off and on?"

"Very close. You do exist, just as those people exist. But not in the form you think."

Amy watched him.

"The true you is much greater than what you see." Then he looked into her eyes. "Amy, you're much greater than you've been taught."

The theater was dark and solemn. The audience was fully entrenched. As the story continued, the suspense built. The audience was intensely silent. People held their breath as a young woman inched toward a closed door.

Suddenly John yelled out. "Watch out! Don't open the door. He's got a knife."

Amy cowered low in her seat. Audience members turned and glared at John.

John was still.

Minutes passed. The audience was again mesmerized. Mourners stood tearfully around a casket. The air was thick with emotion. The audience quietly wiped tears from their eyes.

Suddenly John shouted out. "Don't cry. She's not really dead. She's just acting. It's not real."

A red-faced man whipped around and bared his fist at John. "Get out of here. Now! Or I'll help you out myself."

Amy jumped up and bolted out of the theater. She dashed down the street, soon followed closely by John.

"Why the hell did you do that? Are you trying to get us killed?"

John smiled. "See. Most people don't want to be shaken from their movie. They like the illusion."

Out of breath, Amy stopped. "Well, of course. They went to the theater to enjoy themselves."

"Exactly. People were horrified and sad in there. But they didn't want to be reminded it was all just pretend. Emotions are powerful. And they're very addictive."

"So, what are you telling me?"

"People can be very attached to their movies. And you may be about to find out how angry and threatened they can become when you try to wake them."

That night, in a dimly lit office, a man's hands sifted

through photographs strewn out on a desk. The light from one lone, black desk lamp revealed the faces of the unsuspecting victims---John and Amy. There were photos of them walking through a park, eating at a diner, and winding amidst people on the street.

CHAPTER SEVEN

As Amy dashed into the busy office, the florescent lights wavered and buzzed erratically overhead. Phones rang at every desk. A grim Mr. Lawson argued with two men in black coats. Amy slipped quietly to her desk. The two men walked out without noticing her.

"What's going on?" she whispered to Christine.

"We've been swamped with calls about your article. Most of them angry," Christine said.

"What article?"

Christine turned her computer screen toward Amy. Amy gasped as she read the headline: "Christ Clone Brings Woman Back From the Dead"

"Oh my God!" Amy struggled to breathe. "How did this happen?" She flipped open her laptop. Then she paused, turned, and glared at Mr. Lawson. "My God. He hacked me."

"People are freaking out, Amy." Christine squirmed in her seat. "You've even gotten death threats. I've never seen it like this. Man, Lawson sure got the attention he wanted for this paper."

Without warning, Lawson was on top of them. He

threw photos down on Amy's desk. Amy's eyes widened. The photos were of her and John.

"Do you know who this guy is?" Lawson asked.

"Where did you get these?"

"Do you know this guy's dangerous?"

"Who told you that?" Amy's mind raced. "And who took these pictures?"

Lawson glanced back over her shoulder. Amy looked toward the door. The men were gone.

"Stay away from this guy." he growled.

"What?" Amy gasped. "You're the one who told me to... And you can't tell me who---"

"You're jeopardizing this paper by being associated with this guy. Stay away from him." Terror in his eyes, he dashed off.

"Who took these pictures?" Amy yelled.

She grabbed the photos, knocking the picture of her and her father to the floor. It shattered to pieces. As she gathered up the broken shards of glass, one sharp piece sliced her palm. She grabbed her hand, frantically trying to stop the bleeding.

Amy looked up to see a heavy-set woman barge into the office and grab a nearby worker. Wide-eyed, he pointed at Amy. The woman angrily marched over to Amy.

"Are you the author of this piece of trash? Who do you think you are?" the woman yelled.

Amy fell back in her chair. Everyone in the office froze.

"You're talking with Christ? Death isn't real? We choose it? How dare you." She pounded her fist on Amy's desk. "Death is real, Sweetheart. My husband died a month ago and you've got the nerve to tell me death isn't real? He didn't 'choose' to die. Cancer killed him."

"I'm so sorry," Amy stammered. "I understand your pain, believe me. My father has cancer---"

"Well, I hope some heartless tramp tells you your father is choosing to die." The woman scowled. "That he's choosing to leave you. Then we'll see what you think about death." She towered menacingly over her. "I'm gonna make sure they fire you." She slammed her fist down on Amy's desk and stormed out.

Amy laid her head on her desk. The phone rang. Christine grabbed it. Another angry customer. She quickly hung up. The phone rang...and rang...and rang. A tired and flustered Amy answered it.

"Hello?"

"I know who you are," the voice on the phone menacingly whispered. "I know you're a demon and I know how to defeat you---"

Amy slammed down the phone. "Oh my God. People have gone berserk." She turned to Christine. "I have to get out of here."

"Go!"

As Amy raced out of the building, she noticed a crowd of people forming nearby. They were grumbling and arguing amongst themselves. Suddenly, from behind, a nervous young man grabbed her. His cold bony fingers dug into her arm.

"Hey, do you know the miracle lady who works here?" Amy tried to pull away. "Can you help me find her? I've got this condition...and I know if I could just touch her---"

"I can't help you! I'm sorry." Amy broke free and raced down the street.

As Amy neared the hospital, she saw two men in black walk out and get into a nearby car. Amy ducked behind a tree. The car sped away. Amy quickly slipped into the hospital.

The young woman at the front desk appeared extremely agitated. She signaled Amy over.

"Ms. Michaels we've been receiving complaints about the man you've been in here with."

"My father?"

"No. The other man."

"What? Who complained?"

The nurse glanced around. "I'm sorry. I'm not at liberty to say. But he can't come to this hospital anymore. I'm sorry." She stood and rushed off.

Inside the hospital elevator, Amy's mind was racing. The elevator jolted to a stop, the doors opened and she rushed out. She gasped as she came face to face with John. She quickly dragged him into the empty waiting room nearby.

"What is going on, John? All hell's broken loose. People are going crazy. My boss ran my story. Two men were at the office with pictures of us. What are you keeping from me? Who are those guys?"

"They're just men stuck in their movie." John turned away from her.

"I think they were here at the hospital too. I don't know

70

what they're up to, but something's wrong. That's it! I want my father out of here before something awful happens. If you really can help my dad, do it. Now! Get rid of his cancer."

"You've created quite a drama with your fear, haven't you?"

"Honestly, John. I'm in no mood for any of your lectures right now. Please, just help my dad so we can get out of here."

"I didn't come here to do this for you." He pulled her over to the side. "Sit down." He sat and took Amy's hand. "Let me see the cut on your hand."

"What? How did you know---?" She pulled away her hand. "No. It hurts."

He took her hand and put his hand on top of the cut.

"We don't have time!" Amy shouted.

"Amy. Relax."

Frustrated, Amy sat.

"Now focus," he said. "There's a deeper part of you that knows the truth...that you're perfect and whole. That's how you heal."

Amy struggled to calm herself down.

"See your hand perfect...with no cut." Then he whispered, "None of it is real."

Amy gazed into his eyes. They were deep and commanding. She felt a powerful surge of energy move through her body. He removed his hand from hers. The cut had vanished.

"How did you do that?"

"You did it."

Amy stared at her hand.

"I see you as you really are," he said. "Complete...

perfect. You saw yourself with a cut. I just helped you see the truth." He searched her eyes. "Your body is energy. So, how could it get sick or injured...or die? Remember it's an illusion. Imagine a different picture."

"But that was just a little cut," she cried, fear in her eyes. "My father has cancer."

"There's no difference. It's all energy. It's all what you believe."

Amy stared at him, then swallowed. "Are you Christ?"

There's a deep silence. "Rather than wonder who I am, be in wonder at who YOU are."

John stood. "Now, go to your father."

He followed a shaken Amy into her father's room. The room was still. Deathly pale, Frank's eyes were closed.

"Dad?" she whispered.

No response.

"Dad?" Amy's eyes filled with fear. She turned to John. "I can't do this. Please help him."

"You can do it. Remember what I've shown you." His voice was filled with strength and passion. "Amy, remember who you are."

She felt enveloped by John's presence as she sat by her father's side.

John watched her closely. "There are two large tumors in his lungs."

Amy nodded.

"They're guilt and regret. See him releasing them. Imagine his lungs perfect and healthy."

Amy felt surrounded and filled with a force, an energy she had never felt before. Her hands seemed drawn to her father's chest. She closed her eyes. Every cell in her body seemed to vibrate with powerful energy...with life.

As this energy moved through her and filled her, Amy whispered with tears in her eyes. "Dad? …Can you hear me? Dad? …I love you so much. You've been such a wonderful father. Everything you've done for me has been from love. I know that. Whatever you've done that's made you feel so bad, please know that I love you no matter what. You could never do anything wrong in my eyes. You've been my best friend…and the most wonderful father in the world. … Please don't die. Please, please…stay here with me."

Silence.

Amy gazed up at John. Everything was hazy. She felt lost in another time, another dimension.

John smiled at her. "Let your father rest now."

"But what else can I do?"

"Miracles don't involve struggle."

She was trembling, but at the same time, her senses felt heightened. Amy lovingly kissed her father on his forehead. Then she and John slowly walked out into the hallway.

She was still shaking. "I don't know what I'm doing.

"You did fine."

"What if I didn't do it right? What if my dad doesn't believe he can heal?"

"Believing someone else's will can oppose yours is a problem. That belief can stop you from creating what you want." He stopped her and held her shoulders. "There are millions of different movies. This is your movie. You can create anything you want. Just know deep inside that is true." He took her hand. "Don't doubt. Doubt accomplishes nothing."

For a moment, deep inside Amy could feel his power and wisdom, as if she'd become one with it.

She stared at him. "Is this real?"

"As real as anything else." He smiled at her. "Go on home now. If you stay here, fear and doubt could undo what you just did. Let it be."

As Amy headed back to the office, she braced to face the out-of-control crowd that had gathered there earlier. But as she got closer to the building, no one was there. No angry mob. It was quiet.

She walked back into her office and collapsed at her desk.

"Are you okay?" Christine asked.

"I'm not sure. It's been a long week."

"It got worse after you left. Crazy people were everywhere." Christine stared at her. "Then, all of a sudden...it stopped. People just left."

"I can't believe any of this." Amy shook her head. "If the guy said he was Elvis they would've thought he was just some nut. Mention Christ and they want to kill someone?"

Christine shook her head. "Well, I guess you got that big story you wanted...the one that would get all of New York buzzing."

Amy rolled her eyes.

"Amy, do you really believe this guy is Christ? Here...in New York City? Talking to you?"

Amy sighed. "Y'know. With all the self-proclaimed religious and spiritual people out there, why is this so hard for people to believe?"

"Did he tell you he's Christ?"

"Well...no, not exactly. But he's doing miracle-like things. And he said he was cloned from the Shroud."

"Well Amy, if he's real, like you say. And he's really chosen now to come back. Why would he talk to you instead of a minister or a world leader or someone important?"

"I don't know." Amy looked away. Then turned back. "He chose poor and common people before, didn't he? I'm poor and common. He didn't go to leaders two thousand years ago. And when he did, they didn't believe him. They were expecting some big, powerful guy who would destroy their enemies, right?" Amy became more worked up. "They actually accused him of doing the work of the devil. And then they had him killed. Why would he want to go to the so-called experts?"

"But wouldn't he show himself to the whole world if he was here? Why would he just be in New York?"

"Well." Amy looked around. "He just stayed in one area last time, didn't he? He didn't travel all over the world. ...At least not that we know of." She mumbled, "Come to think of it, I don't know where he goes when he's not with me. He could be anywhere...talking with anyone." She looked at Christine. "And jeez. With all the trouble I've had, I can see why he wouldn't want to show himself to the whole world. It'd probably cause a war."

CHAPTER EIGHT

It was a bright, clear day. Amy anxiously rushed down the street. As she neared the entrance of the hospital, she saw John calming standing nearby. Their eyes met. They moved face to face.

Amy pulled him aside. "You know they don't want you in there."

John smiled and shook his head. "You still don't understand, do you?"

Amy wasn't interested in arguing with him. She turned and dashed into the hospital. John followed.

Once inside, they discovered that the mood was not as bright. The lobby was jammed with people with crutches, canes, walkers, and wheelchairs; some were carrying small children. People were arguing and shoving one another.

The woman at the front desk didn't notice Amy and John enter as she struggled to push people away from her desk. She was arguing with one strong-willed, stocky woman. "We can't admit you just because you have arthritis in your hand."

"I'm here to be healed. I'm not leaving." The stocky woman braced for battle.

The tension in the room was oppressive, like a huge dark storm brewing.

A voice yelled out from the back of the lobby. "My friend's little girl was here dying of cancer. And now she's home like nothing was ever wrong with her."

"Same thing happened to my neighbor's little boy," cried another.

"And my friend actually died of a heart attack here," yelled one man. "She's back home now, healthy as a horse."

The voices sounded like thunder as everyone tried to talk at once. The crowd grew more threatening as they pushed in even tighter.

A man with a dark beard pushed forward and towered over the frightened woman at the desk. "There's something going on in here. We want in."

"There's nothing going on." With terror in her eyes, she tried to push people away from her desk. "We don't have room for you. Go home. All of you."

The crowd refused to leave and pressed even tighter as more people arrived. Amy struggled to squeeze through the masses. John followed her. As they passed by the children, each child smiled and reached out to John. He playfully smiled at them. The distracted parents didn't notice.

Amy was aghast. "So, were these the crowds you were talking about?"

John shook his head. "People still don't know that they are the miracle."

As Amy and John entered Frank's room, Amy's head reeled! Her now vibrant father was sitting on the edge of his bed, the picture of health and radiance. He was busy arguing with a very determined and forceful Maxine.

"My God! Dad!" Amy hastily rushed over to him "Dad. You look great! What's going on? How are you feeling?"

"I feel great." Frank smiled. Then feigning irritation, he glared at Maxine. "Except some crazy woman here keeps poking me with needles."

"Dad. I don't believe this. Look at you!"

A perplexed Dr. Mitchell entered the room. Maxine backed away from Frank. The room was instantly quiet. Amy held her breath and stared expectantly at the doctor. He looked lost as he struggled for words.

"Well," Mitchell stammered. "We've taken three different MRIs and they're all showing up the same. One tumor seems drastically smaller." He gazed into Frank's eyes. "And one tumor...appears to have disappeared completely."

Amy gasped and hugged Frank. "Dad! My God. You did it."

"Well, it's taken it's sweet time," Frank said. "But I guess all that chemo finally paid off."

Amy couldn't let go of him. Grateful tears flowed while she laughed out loud. "I can't believe this, Dad. Maybe we'll actually get you home."

The doctor quickly interrupted. "Let's not get ahead of ourselves. These things have a way of reappearing. We're not convinced there's been any miracles here."

Amy smiled at John as she wiped away tears.

"We've been running tests on him since early this morning," said the baffled Dr. Mitchell. "I think it's better he gets some rest now."

Amy clung to her father even tighter. "But can't we---"

"Look," said Mitchell. "We're not sure what's happened but we don't want any relapses. He needs rest."

Amy nodded. She released her grip on Frank and backed away. The doctor pulled open the curtain between the beds. The other bed was empty.

Amy heart dropped. Her smiled faded. "Where's Mr. Evans?"

"There was nothing more we could do for him. He passed last night." With that, Mitchell turned and walked out.

Seeing the sadness and question in Amy's eyes, John smiled compassionately at her. "People have free will. It's his movie."

Alarmed, Amy turned to her father and grabbed his hand. "Dad, please don't believe you have to die."

"What? I'm not going to die, Honey. Don't let those doctors scare you."

"No Dad. Don't believe you have to die."

"Well, Amy. We all have to die sometime. It's a part of life."

"No Dad. I don't believe that anymore. We need to stop believing in death. It's not real. And it causes too much pain." Amy was surprised by her own words.

"Well of course it causes pain. If it didn't, people would be doing it more often. Amy, I was a cop, remember? I've seen death. It's very real."

Amy took a deep breath, trying to calm herself down. "Okay Dad. We'll talk about it later." She hugged him. "I'll be back tomorrow. I'm so happy you're better."

As John and Amy walked out into the hallway, her eyes flooded with gratitude and joy.

"Thank you. Thank you. Thank you."

John smiled. "I didn't do anything."

"You healed my dad."

John shook his head. Amy pulled away.

"Amy, why are you so afraid to see who you are?"

"But I didn't... It couldn't be... It was because of you. I...I can't even boil water."

John laughed. "Miracles don't require boiling water."

"But...why didn't all the cancer go away then?"

"You didn't completely believe it was possible."

"But I wanted all the cancer gone."

John paused. "You don't always get what you want. You always get what you believe."

"So, I believed the cancer was still there?"

John nodded. "Old pictures can be tough to let go of. You've all believed in illness and death for so long, you can't even imagine a world without them."

"Well, I need to try again," she said as she spun around with determination and headed back. "I want the cancer gone."

John grabbed her.

"Be patient with yourself. You may still see the old picture for awhile until the new belief becomes more real to you."

"I need to know how to change it all so we can get my dad out of here."

"I'll tell you the secret," John said as they turned and entered the elevator. "You put too much focus on the problem. You think about it, talk about it, struggle with it. That only feeds it energy, which makes it bigger and stronger. To change anything, first become quiet. Gently lift your energy and attention off the old picture. Then choose a new picture and put your attention and belief on that one instead." John noticed Amy was trying to grasp the concept. "If you don't like the picture you're painting...stop painting it. Paint a new one. Choose again."

She stared in disbelief. "It sounds so simple."

"It is. But most people are addicted to their problems and dramas. They think creating a new picture is too much work. Or worse, they think a different picture is impossible."

The elevator doors opened, and they stepped out. There was still a madhouse in the lobby.

"These people need to know about this," Amy said as they struggled to squeeze through the crowd.

John smiled at her.

Amy shook her head. "Don't look at me."

"You're the writer. I thought you wanted people to know the truth. Well, the truth according to John anyway. That's all I can tell them."

"One measly article gets me death threats and you want me to write more? You see how worked up people get. We'd just be asking for trouble."

"Is that what you're asking for?" He smiled at her. "This world's been run by fear for too long, don't you think?"

CHAPTER NINE

As Amy and John walked toward her apartment, the night felt eerily ominous. Amy wanted to be excited about her dad but something inside felt wrong again. One streetlight flickered in the dark, making the strangely moving shadows cast on the sidewalk appear to be warning them to turn around---like something was lurking ahead.

Then a chill ran up Amy's spine. Two men in black stood outside Amy's building.

"Oh no," she whispered to John. "Let's not go this way."

John shook his head. "Still full of fear, huh? I thought I'd made more progress with you."

"I think those are the same guys I saw at the office. ...Who are they?"

"Men from Washington," John said.

"You know them?"

"I know who they are."

"I don't want something bad happening now, John. My dad's better. I can get him home soon. Please, don't mess with these guys."

But John continued on.

As Amy and John moved closer, the men approached

them. One man pushed out and flashed a badge at John. "You need to come with us."

Amy stepped forward defiantly. "For what reason?"

"Easy Mama Bear." John pulled her back. "It's okay."

The men grabbed John by his arms and pulled him away. As Amy started after them, John quickly shot a look her.

"Fear creates fear."

Amy watched helplessly as they pushed John into the back of a black car and sped off. She raced up to her apartment. Once inside, Amy picked up the phone. Then slammed it down. She walked to the refrigerator and opened the door. Then slammed it shut. She paced by the window and glanced out. She picked up the phone again, then paused and slammed it down. Frustrated, she threw herself face down onto her sofa.

In a dimly lit room, two men in black sat across the room from John, never taking their eyes off him. One fidgeted with a black and gold ring on his hand.

A third man entered the room and pulled one of the men aside. "There's nothing. No I.D. No fingerprints on that glass. Nothing."

The man turned and sat down directly across from John. John sat quietly.

"What are you doing in New York?" the man asked.

John remained quiet.

"It's our job to keep track of potential problems...and make sure those problems go away."

John stared into the man's eyes.

Uncomfortable with John's intense gaze, the man stood

up. "We do have the authority to keep you here until we get answers."

John smiled. "You have no authority over me."

The man sneered at John. "You don't know who you're dealing with."

John just looked at him.

The man studied John. "What's your connection with the girl?"

Suddenly there was a knock.

Amy was jolted out of her sleep by a knock. Disoriented at first, she got up from the sofa and staggered to the door. She peeked through the security hole, gasped, and threw open the door. John stood there with a smile on his face.

"John! What happened? Where did they take you? What did they do to you?"

John entered. "First things first. I would love something to eat."

"How can a deity be so interested in food?!" she wailed.

"One of the pleasures of this movie." He walked to the refrigerator and helped himself to all he could carry.

"John! Where were you? Who are they? What happened?"

"How can you have so much fear in your voice when I'm standing right in front of you?"

"I was worried out of my mind."

"Then you still don't know who I am." John sighed. "And after all I've shown you."

"Okay. I admit. I'm not as advanced as you are. Cut me some slack, will you?" Amy paced. "Like it or not, I've grown rather attached to you. And I don't like it when people I know get dragged away in the night by strange men."

"Well, actually I was impressed that you found me. Maybe you're more advanced than you think."

"What? I found you?"

He nodded. "And I'm assuming you heard everything they said."

"That was real? You were really in that room? I thought that was a dream."

John sighed and shook his head. "Dream. Movie. What's the difference?"

Amy paused. Then she snapped back.

"Wait a minute. If that was really happening, how did you get away?"

"They thought they locked me in a room with walls," he said. "I didn't see any walls."

Amy's head spun. "Why did they take you?"

"They're afraid of anyone they can't control or intimidate."

A look of bewilderment then indignation crossed Amy's face.

CHAPTER TEN

Amy and John stepped through the front doors of the hospital and into the lobby. Amy stopped…stunned. It was now quiet and empty.

"Where are all the people?" Amy gasped. "What happened to all the crazies?"

"You want them back?" John asked.

"No! …But where are they? What happened? There were at least fifty people here yesterday."

"I'm not interested in drama …or crowds." John looked at her. "But if you want them back, that can be arranged."

"What?"

He smiled. "It's my movie."

An orange glow from the setting sun streamed through Frank's hospital room window as Amy and John helped him pack up his belongings.

John smiled at Frank. "I'm glad to hear the cancer's gone and you're feeling better."

"Well, they said it's gone into remission," Frank said. "They seem to think it could come back."

"Hmm. What do you think?" John studied him.

Frank gazed at Amy. "Well. My daughter here is trying to convince me I could be completely healed and live a long healthy life."

"Wise daughter," John said as he smiled at Amy.

Uncomfortable with the attention, Amy interrupted. "Okay you guys. I have to go sign some papers so we can get you out of here. Will you two behave yourselves while I'm gone?"

John grinned mischievously. Amy returned a warm and grateful smile, then dashed out of the room.

The two men sat silently. Frank stared at the ground.

Finally, Frank looked up. "My daughter tells me you helped her through all of this."

They locked eyes.

Frank's voice trembled, on the verge of tears. "Thank you."

John nodded. There was a long silence.

John caught Frank's eyes. "Carrying guilt and regret will eat you up again, you know."

Frank paused. "Excuse me?"

"Why haven't you told her the truth?"

Frank sat up straight.

"Why haven't you told her you found her on your doorstep?" John continued.

Frank's breathing quickened. He looked around to see if Amy was nearby. "How do you know that?" His eyes narrowed as he nervously stared at John. "Who are you?"

"I'm here to help."

Frank pulled back.

"Don't worry," John said. "I'm not going to say anything. But you need to stop keeping this secret. It's eating you up."

Frank quietly stared at the ground. Tears were forming in his eyes. Then he looked up and searched John's eyes.

"After all these years." He sighed. "She was so small and helpless. I'd seen what happened to abandoned children. They got lost in the system. I didn't want that to happen to her."

Frank looked around again to see if Amy was coming. "I couldn't tell her when she was little because if it had gotten out, they would've taken her away from me."

Frank squirmed.

"I moved to New York so no one would know. If I had stayed in Washington, people would've been suspicious. A single cop suddenly shows up with a baby?" He stared at the ground. "Here, people believed I was a grieving widower with a baby daughter. I even fixed my files so they wouldn't know. So they wouldn't bother me. Me…a regular, by-the-book cop who always followed the rules."

They stared at each other. John smiled compassionately, but knowingly.

Frank hung his head. "I was so alone at the time. She's all I've ever had. I didn't want to lose her."

"Why haven't you told her now?"

"I don't want her to hate me. I don't know who put her on my doorstep. What if she wants to know why I didn't take her somewhere so they could find her real mother? It's too late now. There's no way to find her. I've messed up her life because I didn't want to lose her."

"She won't hate you. And she won't leave you. She loves you. But she deserves to know."

Silence. Frank stared at the mysterious man. "How did you know?"

More silence.

"You a cop?"

John shook his head. "You worked on a case I was involved in thirty years ago."

"Thirty years ago? What case was that?"

"You were a police officer in Washington at the time. Someone broke into a lab. They stole a piece of cloth."

Frank pondered. "Yeah. I remember that lab. The guy wouldn't let us in." He looked off into the distance. "I remember they had pictures of the..." Then he snapped back. "Cloth? They stole cloth? Was it from that Shroud?"

John nodded.

"I knew it had something to do with that Shroud." Then Frank's brow furled. He turned to John. "How were you involved in that? You can't be that old."

John stared at the doorway. "I'm what came of that piece of cloth."

Frank looked puzzled.

"They were experimenting with cloning at the time." John studied Frank carefully. "They cloned me from that cloth."

"Cloning?" Frank asked. "What? But if that cloth was from the Shroud..." The color suddenly drained from Frank's face.

Amy returned.

CHAPTER ELEVEN

There was no moon out that night, which made Amy's quiet neighborhood seem even darker. Only the occasional streetlamp lit their way as John and Amy walked down the street.

"Thanks for helping me take my dad home. He's so happy to be in his own bed again."

Amy could no longer contain herself. She threw her arms in the air and spun around. "We did it! We really did it. It works. I can't believe it. We healed my dad." She looked into John's eyes. "It's real, isn't it? Everything you've been telling me. It's real. He's really healed."

John nodded.

Amy laughed. "Did you see those doctors? They don't know what to think. They expected him to be dead by now." Thinking back, she smiled. "And my poor father doesn't know what to make of you. He couldn't say two words. Maybe you can help explain things to him?"

Amy stopped and stared at John with grateful, excited, deep wide eyes. "I want to know more. Show me---"

SUDDENLY WITHOUT WARNING, A MAN IN BLACK BOLTED OUT OF THE DARK, FIRED A GUN POINT BLANK INTO JOHN'S STOMACH, AND RACED OFF.

Amy screamed. John sank to the ground. A car screeched and sped away.

"John!" Amy cried. "Oh my God! John!"

She dropped to the ground and held him. Blood poured from John's stomach. She tried desperately to stop the bleeding.

"John! What do I do?!"

Curious faces peered out of their apartment windows. Sirens screamed in the distance. Amy struggled to take a deep breath, then placed both her hands on his stomach.

"Stop bleeding!" she yelled. "Stop now! You're whole and perfect. Stop bleeding."

John struggled to look up at her. For the first time ever, Amy saw fear and pain in his eyes.

"Oh my God! John!" she screamed. "It's not working. Why don't you stop this?"

She frantically looked around. "Someone help us!" she screamed.

John looked at her with sadness in his eyes, then closed his eyes...and died.

"John!" she screamed. "No! No! You can't die! You said death's not real!"

An ambulance screeched up. Paramedics jumped out, lifted John onto a gurney and into the ambulance. Staggering in shock, Amy tried to get into the back of the ambulance. A man shoved her away. On his hand was a black and gold ring. The doors slammed. The ambulance sped off.

"Wait!" she cried out after them. "Where are you taking him? John!"

She started running after the ambulance. She ran and ran and ran. Tears streamed down her face. She was splattered with blood. There were no cabs in sight. She ran blocks to the hospital. Out of breath, she burst into the emergency room. A startled nurse stood near by.

Amy grabbed her. "My friend..." She struggled to catch her breath. "They just picked up...my friend. Please. ...Where is he?"

"Calm down, Miss." The nurse backed away from her and grabbed the register. "What's your friend's name?"

"John," she cried. "His name is John."

"John what?"

"John! John! John!"

The nurse paused. "What did you do tonight, Dear? Meth? Heroin?"

Amy cried hysterically. "He was shot. They just took him."

The nurse shook her head. "No one's come in here with a gunshot wound. Not tonight."

"That's impossible. They took him. He has to be here."

"I'm sorry, Miss. Let's get you in---"

"Let me look!" Amy screamed as she tried to run through the inside emergency doors.

"Hey!" The nurse grabbed her. "You can't go in there." They struggled. "Security!"

A security guard rushed in and grabbed Amy.

"He has to be here. Please. Let me look."

Amy broke free. She frantically looked around, then dodging them, ran back out to the street. She screamed for a taxi. A cab screeched to a stop. Amy jumped in. A young man leaned over the front seat.

"Where's the next hospital?" Amy yelled.

Shocked, the young man spun forward. "A few minutes from here."

"Take me there. Please. Hurry!"

Tires squealing, they sped off. Amy sat in the back seat, trembling. There was still a huge amount of blood on her hands and clothes.

"This can't be happening." She struggled to take deep breaths as she ranted out loud. "No fear. No fear. No fear." Then she burst into tears and screamed, "I'm not that strong. This is too much. I can't do this!"

A look of terror filled the driver's face. He raced even faster toward the hospital. Amy stared out the window, her face stained with tears.

As the cab screeched to a halt at the emergency entrance of the hospital, Amy jumped out. "Wait here. Please. I need to check---"

The cab raced off.

Amy burst into the E.R, nearly colliding with a nurse.

"I'm looking for my friend. He was shot in the stomach."

"He didn't come in here," the nurse said.

"He has to be here!" Amy screamed.

The nurse pulled back and shook her head. "No gun shot wounds. I've been here all night."

"Oh God. This has to be a dream." Amy turned and stared at the floor. "Please, let this be a dream."

She took a deep breath and turned to the nurse. "Could you please, please help me? I need to find my friend. They picked him up. I don't know where they took him."

The nurse paused, studied her face, then picked up the phone. "Which hospitals have you checked?"

Amy unlocked the door to her apartment. She stood in the doorway, in the dark. She walked in, looked around her lonely apartment, dragged herself into her bedroom and collapsed onto her bed. She lay sobbing in the dark.

"John. Come back."

Days later, Amy walked alone through the park, her head hung low. A cold wind whipped fiercely, stinging her eyes and face. She pulled her coat tightly around her. The hope that her father's friends in the department would find out what happened was slowly fading.

Late into the night, Amy sat staring out her apartment window as a hard rain tormented the city.

Amy sat at her office desk, mindlessly pushing a pencil back and forth. Then staring at her computer, she slowly punched one letter at a time. Then she paused, hit the backspace key again and again, and erased everything she had typed.

Days later, Amy sat beside a fountain in the park. Tears in her eyes, she gazed soulfully at the water. Then she rose and walked down the street. Empty and alone, her eyes never left the ground.

That night Amy stood staring at her refrigerator. Then she turned and walked out of her apartment.

Amy and Frank sat at his dining table. He watched with concern as Amy pushed food around on her plate. Frank took a deep breath. "Amy? I don't know if this is the best time...but I've been needing to talk with you."

CHAPTER TWELVE

Standing at her desk at the office, Amy packed her things into a box. Loitering next to her, Mr. Lawson, his toupee now gone from his balding head, was pulling those same items back out of the box.

"But I've given everyone a raise," Lawson said with a trace of panic in his voice. "And they have flexible hours now. Ms. Adams here can even leave early if she needs to get her kids. I've made it all better. C'mon, just stay. …How about one more piece and we'll see how it goes?" He looked at Christine. "Will you please get her to stay?"

Amy glanced around to see calm and relaxed people working at their computers. Colorful items, family photos and plants on every desk.

Lawson pointed around the room. "See, everyone's happy."

Co-workers looked up at Amy. They knew who was responsible for this remarkable transformation.

Amy continued to pull items from her desk drawers and put them in the box as Lawson continued to pull items back out of the box.

"Okay. Name your price," he pleaded.

Amy finally stopped and handed him a plant. "It'll be okay, Mr. Lawson. You have good people here. Let them do their jobs and the paper will be fine."

Lawson hung his head, turned, and carrying the plant, slowly walked away.

Christine smiled at Amy. "He knows you're the one who skyrocketed the subscriptions for this paper. Who knew your story would have such an impact on so many people? I guess the paper's willing to run another one after the huge sales from that first one.

Christine paused and looked at Amy. "Did you know your story brought in the highest sales in this paper's history? ...I guess there are more positive people out there hungry for hopeful information than there are angry people who want to blame and destroy. Thanks to you, we get to write a lot more interesting and inspirational stories now. It's amazing how many people are out there talking about these types of things and sharing unusual experiences. I had no idea. And people still want more!"

Christine looked fondly at Amy. "Thank you for everything you've done. I don't understand all of it, but a lot of people seem to resonate with your story. So, something good is coming from it all.

Amy smiled at her.

Christine helped her pack. "What are you going to do now?"

Amy hesitated. "I don't know."

"I can't believe you actually quit."

"You said yourself I'm better than this." Amy packed with determination.

"What about money? How will you live?"

Amy shrugged. "I just know I have to do this. Something

is still missing. My life is meant to be more...I can feel it. I need to know what that is. I'm not afraid anymore."

They continued clearing Amy's desk.

Christine hesitated. "So, he's not your real father?"

Amy whipped around. "He IS my father."

"But he's not your birth father?"

"It doesn't matter. He's my father."

"Are you going to try to find your real parents?"

"I don't know."

There was an uncomfortable silence.

"I'm sorry about your friend," whispered Christine.

Amy lowered her head.

"I'm sure he's in a better place," Christine added.

"Yeah." Then under her breath, Amy whispered, "I wonder where that is."

She hugged Christine, picked up the box, and walked out.

Amy entered her apartment carrying a bag of groceries. She stopped and stared at the refrigerator, then she looked up and called out. "Sorry, John. I never learned how to work this thing."

She stood with her hand on the refrigerator door and closed her eyes. Moments later, she pulled open the door. Inside sat one, small, solitary muffin. She gasped. Her mouth dropped open.

Suddenly there was a knock on the door. Amy continued to stare at the refrigerator, oblivious to the knock.

There was another knock.

Still in shock, Amy mindlessly dropped the bag of

groceries down on the counter and staggered to the front door. She opened it to find...

John!

She gasped in disbelief, unable to speak. Then she whispered, "Am I having a dream?"

"Movie. Dream," he said. "What's the difference?"

Amy threw her arms around him. Tears flowed down her face.

John paused, then glanced over her shoulder at the lone muffin in the open refrigerator. He smiled. "Well...it's a start."

Amy smiled as she stepped back and wiped away tears. "A start? It's amazing. Considering I'm a mere mortal."

"Is that what you think?"

They stood staring at one another.

Amy quietly brooded. "I called you back."

"I heard you."

"Why didn't you come?"

"I'm here."

"What took you so long? I've been in a lot of pain."

"Then you don't remember who you are."

"I thought you died."

John shook his head.

Amy stared at the floor. "I kept thinking...and hoping... that maybe you... But it got harder and harder to believe... That night was really convincing, you know?"

"Good movies usually are."

"Those men have been watching outside for a long time," she said.

"I saw them. They're stubborn." John smiled mischievously. "And very attached to their movie. I'll wait 'til they believe I'm good and dead. Then I'll let them see me. That should shake 'em up."

Amy quietly smiled. John walked to the fridge, picked up the muffin and closed the refrigerator door.

She watched him carefully. "So now what?"

He pulled the muffin apart and handed half to Amy. "Aren't you going to write?" His half of the muffin was already in his mouth.

"Write? I don't want to go through any of that again."

"Well," he winked. "There's always movies."

"What do you mean?"

"Why don't you write a movie? People don't take movies as seriously as they do their books."

Amy stared at him.

"People don't go to war over movies," he said. "Only over books. They believe movies are make-believe. They believe only their books are holy and divinely inspired."

"But I don't want to be harassed by angry people."

"Do what the others did. Only use your first name."

"The others?"

"You know," he grinned. "Matthew, Mark, Luke..."

Amy was not amused.

"The gospel according to Amy," he teased.

"Using the word gospel? Hmm. I don't know."

"Well, you can use my name. I'm not afraid to say what I believe. How about 'The Truth According to John'?"

Amy smiled fondly at him. "It has a certain ring to it." Then she paused and looked at the floor. "So now what? Are you going away?"

"No. I have work to do."

"Really!" her head snapped up. "You're not leaving again?"

"I never really left you the first time," he said.

"Will we talk any more?"

"It's your movie."

"Good." She grabbed the handle on the refrigerator door. "Now talk to me about this refrigerator."

He paused. "Amy, there's something I haven't told you."

"Oh no." She quivered and backed away.

"You said you wanted to know---" he started.

"I changed my mind! I don't wanna know anything more. I'm done learning."

She walked away, avoiding eye contact. She glanced out the window, then looked back at him.

"Don't you think I've learned enough for one lifetime?" She held up her half of the muffin. "Can't you just give me a gold star and say we're done?"

John smiled.

Amy wasn't smiling. "If any of that was an example of how you're going to teach me, I'm done. I can't handle any more."

"After a while, you'll see there's nothing to handle."

Amy looked away. "Are you going to walk through walls or something?"

He looked around. "You see walls?"

"Well. What is it then?"

"The reason for the cloning."

Amy stared at him.

"The scientists who did the cloning were hoping to change the world."

"How?"

"By bringing in someone who could show them a higher truth about life."

"You?" she asked.

John carefully watched her face. "Before they could complete their work, they realized the men who were bent on destroying it had gotten too close. So, they hid what they'd created...all over the world. Those intent on destroying it have been searching ever since. Searching. Watching."

"All over the world?"

"You realize that if they could clone one being from the Shroud...they could clone two...or ten...or hundreds."

Amy reeled. "Oh my God. You mean there's others like you out there? But... Where?"

"They're out there. Most of them just don't realize who they are yet. They still believe what they've been taught to believe...that they're victims…instead of creators of their movies. They'll remember though. Like I did. In time, they'll all realize who they are."

John watched her. "Amy, the people who did the cloning could manipulate the DNA any way they wanted. They could alter the appearance...the skin, eyes, hair color...even the gender."

Amy stared at him. "What are you telling me? That each one could look completely different? And there are male and female?!"

John nodded. "They hid some of the children they'd created in adoption centers. Slipped into fertility clinics to inject eggs."

Silence.

"And in some cases...left babies on doorsteps."

Amy staggered back against the refrigerator. The muffin dropped to the floor.

"Those men haven't been watching me," he said.

"They've been following you for years. They haven't been sure about you...until now."

John looked intensely at Amy. His deep eyes seemed to hold all of eternity.

"It's time you remember who you are. The world is about to change. We have work to do."

The End
And a New Beginning...

ABOUT THE AUTHOR

Pamala Oslie is an author, consultant, radio show host, professional intuitive psychic, medium, and aura expert. Pamala has appeared on ABC, CBS, NBC, The Dr. Oz Show, The View, The Ricki Lake Show, Coast to Coast with George Noory, Hallmark's Home & Family, Gaia, many other television and radio shows, and in numerous national magazines. She has a very extensive clientele, including many celebrities. Pam has spoken at the TEDx Talks, the International Forum on New Science, Fortune 500 companies, and many seminars for professionals in the psychology, education, health fields and more. She was awarded the Holistic Transformational Leader of the Year Award by the Global Association of Holistic Psychotherapy and Coaching.

Made in United States
North Haven, CT
20 October 2021

10452557R00063